MW00527579

"Madelin

"Oh, Jake," she moaned. "Don't you understand? I wanted to make love to you! I—I still do!"

"Is that so bad?"

"Yes." She gasped. "I don't even know you. And thank God you don't know me!"

"You don't know what you're saying, Madeline," he said softly. "I want to know you in every way a man can know a woman."

She gripped the front of his shirt and choked back a sob. "You'd only be disappointed," she told him. "I like you, Jake. I like you very much. Don't ask more from me."

Dear Reader:

The spirit of the Silhouette Romance Homecoming Celebration lives on as each month we bring you six books by continuing stars!

And we have a galaxy of stars planned for 1988. In the coming months, we're publishing romances by many of your favorite authors such as Annette Broadrick, Sondra Stanford and Brittany Young. Beginning in January, Debbie Macomber has written a trilogy designed to cure any midwinter blues. And that's not all—during the summer, Diana Palmer presents her most engaging heros and heroines in a trilogy that will be sure to capture your heart.

Your response to these authors and other authors of Silhouette Romances has served as a touchstone for us, and we're pleased to bring you more books with Silhouette's distinctive medley of charm, wit and—above all—romance.

I hope you enjoy this book and the many stories to come. Come home to romance—for always!

Sincerely,

Tara Hughes
Senior Editor
Silhouette Books

STELLA BAGWELL

Madeline's Song

Silhouette *Romance*

Published by Silhouette Books New York

America's Publisher of Contemporary Romance

To my son, Jason, with love;
my struggle to have him
inspired this book.

SILHOUETTE BOOKS
300 E. 42nd St., New York, N.Y. 10017

Copyright © 1987 by Stella Bagwell

All rights reserved, including the right to reproduce
this book or portions thereof in any form whatsoever.
For information address Silhouette Books,
300 E. 42nd St., New York, N.Y. 10017

ISBN: 0-373-08543-5

First Silhouette Books printing November 1987

All the characters in this book are fictitious. Any
resemblance to actual persons, living or dead, is
purely coincidental.

SILHOUETTE, SILHOUETTE ROMANCE and colophon
are registered trademarks of the publisher.

America's Publisher of Contemporary Romance

Printed in the U.S.A.

Books by Stella Bagwell

Silhouette Romance

Golden Glory #469
Moonlight Bandit #485
A Mist on the Mountain #510
Madeline's Song #543

STELLA BAGWELL

is a small-town girl and an incurable romantic—a combination she feels enhances her writing. When she isn't at her typewriter she enjoys reading, listening to music, sketching pencil drawings and sewing her own clothes. Most of all she enjoys exploring the outdoors with her husband and young son.

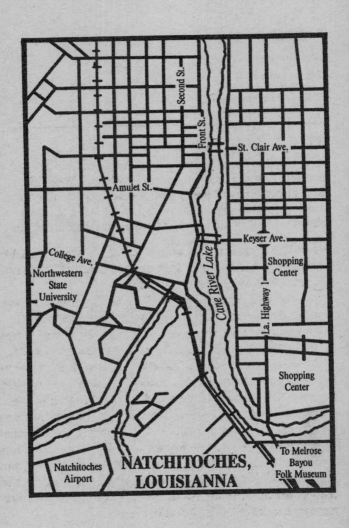

NATCHITOCHES, LOUISIANNA

Chapter One

Madeline Beaumont was about four blocks away from her destination when her little Fiat coughed, lunged, then quietly rolled to a halt against the curb.

Cursing desperately under her breath, she turned the key. Nothing happened. The car was dead. Totally dead!

Moaning with frustration, she ripped the key from the ignition, then fell with a tired thump against the seat. She was going to have to walk, Madeline realized. It would be at least an hour before her mother would be home, and she had no intention of paying a tow truck to pull her four blocks.

It was April and already fiercely hot. Louisiana was known for its sultry weather, and the city of Natchitoches was no exception. Living in Missouri for seven years had made her almost forget the unbearable heat. Almost, but not quite. With the air conditioning shut off, the interior of the car quickly became stifling, and she reached simultaneously for the door latch and her handbag.

Madeline could feel a fine film of sweat breaking out under her clothes as she locked the doors, then opened the trunk. She would take only her leather shoulder bag. There was no need to contend with any of the heavier suitcases.

Flowers were already blooming profusely, and the lawns Madeline passed were thick and green. Under other circumstances she would have enjoyed walking the remaining distance to her mother's house, but not after driving several hundred miles. She was exhausted and wanted only to rest.

Sighing, she began walking south on Second Street, her white heels clicking against the hot pavement. The sun beat down on her thick, copper-colored hair and she was thankful she had wound it up at the back of her head. If she had left it hanging to her shoulders she would have been doubly uncomfortable.

Pausing to catch her breath, she shifted the heavy bag to her other shoulder and looked around to get her bearings. The Fort Claiborne guest house stood to her left, its two and a half stories a perfect example of traditional Louisiana architecture. The sight of it made her realize she had farther to go than she had first thought.

Madeline had taken only a few steps more when a motorcycle passed by. It came to a screeching halt about a hundred feet in front of her. She watched the driver make a wide arc in the street and head back in her direction.

"Do you need a ride, miss?" he asked after making another skidding stop right beside her.

She hesitated just long enough to glance at the driver of the motorcycle. He was in his thirties and had thick coffee-colored hair and a wide, reckless grin.

Feeling wary, she looked at him coolly. "I don't accept lifts from strangers," she told him.

He studied her intently for a moment. She was some looker, he had to admit, but there was a haughtiness about her he could well do without. She was wearing a straight white skirt and a royal-blue blouse that was cut very low in back. Even at this distance he could see the skin of her shoulders was faintly sprinkled with light freckles and looked deliciously soft.

"If you're worried about the skirt, you can sit sidesaddle and I'll drive slowly," he suggested.

Madeline frowned at his impertinence and started to walk on. "No, thank you. I'm only going as far as Amulet Street. It's no problem."

Still astride the motorcycle, he walked it beside her. She had one of those regal-looking faces, he decided, as well as a faintly squared jaw, full lips, a thin nose and almond-shaped eyes that looked green or maybe hazel. They were framed with outrageously long lashes. All in all, she was damn sexy, he admitted to himself.

"My name is Jake Hunter," he told her, then paused to give her the opportunity to disclose her name.

Instead she said, "Well, Jake Hunter, do you make a habit of trying to pick up women on the street?"

He chuckled in spite of her sharp tone. "It all depends on the woman," he answered.

As she glared at him he got back on the motorcycle, turned the ignition key, and sped off with a loud roar.

Madeline drew a relieved breath as she watched him ride down the street. He tossed her a careless wave, but she ignored it. Men like him construed any kind of action as an encouragement, and the sooner this man was out of sight, the better she would like it.

A few minutes later she neared the old courthouse and was gazing lovingly at its spiral staircase when the sound of a car broke her concentration.

Looking away from the carefully restored building and glancing across the narrow street, she saw a white Cadillac convertible, at least ten years old, parked across from her. Much to her dismay, the driver was beckoning to her!

She blinked and then gasped in astonishment. It was the driver of the motorcycle. He had obviously changed modes of transportation, but how and when? He had been gone only a few minutes!

"Since you didn't like my bike I thought you'd be more impressed with my car."

Madeline gripped the strap of her shoulder bag as he walked across the street toward her. He had an athletic body. He was at least six feet tall, had broad shoulders, and strong-looking thigh muscles that strained against his faded jeans as he walked.

With a certain amount of effort Madeline moved her gaze from him to the car. It looked shiny but extremely well-used. Did he actually expect her to be impressed? Laughter bubbled in her throat, and she couldn't think of ever being in a more ridiculous situation.

"Look, I really don't need a ride. I thought I made that clear."

"Come on," he said encouragingly. "That's your Fiat broken down back there, isn't it?"

She looked directly at him, trying to decide if he was just an observant, sincere man, or some kind of psycho hiding behind a handsome face. She had to admit he was rather nice-looking with clear gray eyes and expressive lips. He was a Southerner; it was evident in his drawl. She didn't think he was from Louisiana, though. Probably Georgia, she thought.

"Yes, that is my Fiat," she admitted reluctantly. "But it will be perfectly fine until I get someone to tow it in for me."

"Tow it!" he repeated with mock horror. "Why do that when you've got a great mechanic right here in front of you? I'll take a look at it. It's probably something very minor."

He grinned widely at Madeline, making her spine stiffen in outrage. "Unless it's just out of gas," he added.

"I do know what the *E* stands for on the fuel gauge," she informed him angrily.

"Good." He smiled and winked at her. "I knew you were a smart woman before I ever saw the front of you."

She wanted to groan with sheer frustration but clenched her teeth to prevent it. He tossed the keys to the Cadillac carelessly in the air and then caught them again.

"Ready?" he asked.

Madeline told herself she should keep walking, but she knew he would only pester her the remaining distance if she did. Surely he was harmless in spite of his forwardness, she tried to assure herself.

Coming to a sudden decision, she stepped around him and walked sedately to the Cadillac.

He was there to open the door for her before she even had the chance to find the latch, and once seated, she watched him curiously as he jogged around to his side of the car. Could it be the man had actually learned a few manners somewhere in his past?

The leather upholstery was hot from the glaring sunshine and Madeline shifted uncomfortably on the seat and crossed her legs.

Jake Hunter openly eyed the movement of her shapely calves and wondered if the rest of her body, hidden beneath those expensive clothes, looked as good as her legs.

"What happened when the car died? Was it making a noise, or were there any warning lights on?"

Madeline looked at him intently as the powerful Cadillac crawled along the street. She noticed that he was wearing a ring on one hand. On closer inspection she realized the ring was an expensive one, not flashy but very tasteful and masculine-looking. A gold watch encircled his left wrist, and

Madeline didn't have to look twice to know that it was the real thing.

She wondered if she was in the company of a thief. It seemed logical; he wore well-used clothes but expensive jewelry. Perhaps he was a car thief and wanted to steal her Fiat. The idea made her laugh to herself. The man couldn't be a car thief and drive this huge, conspicuous thing around.

"Er—nothing really happened. All at once it just stopped. When I tried the key it was dead, as if the battery had failed," she explained.

"Hmm, I'm not really up on foreign cars, but I'd say it was an electrical problem. You gotta have a spark to bring on the combustion in any of them."

Madeline's eyebrows lifted at his words. Was he talking about engines or—

"Yes, well, I hope you're right," she murmured.

It took only two or three minutes to reach her car. Madeline unlocked the driver's door and showed him how the car reacted when she turned the key.

"Release the hood," he instructed.

She obeyed and he began inspecting the engine. After a minute or two he came back around to where Madeline still sat behind the wheel.

"I can't find anything up there," he said. "Would you mind scooting over?"

She moved to the opposite side of the seat, and he bent over to look under the dashboard. Apparently he couldn't see very well in that position so he lay down on his back and poked his head beneath the steering column.

Madeline was just about to ask what he expected to find when his left hand reached up and turned the key on. Sparks flew and he immediately twisted it off.

"What is it?" she asked anxiously. "Have you found the problem?"

"Just a minute."

Finally he wriggled out from beneath the dashboard and stepped back out on the ground. "Try it now," he instructed.

She did, and the engine started instantly. For a moment she sat there in shock, and then a smile lit her face as she looked at him. Andrew would never have been able to do this. "I can't believe it! You're a genius!"

He grinned. She was damn beautiful when she smiled, just as he knew she would be.

"Not really," he conceded. "I just found a wire that had jolted loose. It had the same effect as turning the key off."

"Well, I certainly thank you," she said sincerely. She reached for her handbag. "What do I owe you?"

"Not a thing, ma'am. The pleasure was mine."

"Oh, but I'd have had to pay a garage if you hadn't come by," she insisted. She felt embarrassed now for being so cool with him before, especially since he was being so generous now.

He shrugged, thinking money was the very last thing he'd like to have from her. "Just don't ever pass me by if you see me broken down."

She nodded. "Of course I wouldn't. And thank you once again."

As he lifted his hand in farewell, Jake realized he still didn't even know this woman's name. He was about to call after her, but abruptly she pulled away from the curb.

A strange sense of disappointment hit Madeline as she realized that Jake Hunter had been the first man in a long, long while to spark any kind of feeling in her, even if that feeling had merely been irritation. Sighing, she looked in her rearview mirror and saw he was climbing back into the white Cadillac.

Oh well, she thought, that would probably be her last glimpse of Jake Hunter. But somehow she knew she would be a long time in forgetting him. Only minutes later Madeline realized she couldn't have been more wrong. As she flipped on the blinker and turned into her mother's driveway, the white Cadillac was right behind her. In fact, it was more than right behind her—it was pulling into the driveway, too!

They both jumped out of their cars, speaking at the same time.

"You didn't have to—"

"What are—"

He looked at her with puzzled curiosity. "Your name wouldn't happen to be Madeline, would it?"

She couldn't have been more flabbergasted. "Why, yes, it is," she said. "But how did you know? Why are you stopping here?"

"Because I live here. I rent the guest house from your mother. Celia's a lovely woman I might add."

"Rent! I didn't know she'd taken in a renter!"

He shrugged, seemingly unmoved by her confusion. "She probably thought it wasn't important enough to mention."

"But—"

"Do you have luggage?" he asked. "I'll help you with it."

Feeling as though the wind had been taken out of her sails, she slowly followed him.

"Yes, I do." Her mind in a whirl, she unlocked the trunk to display four large suitcases.

"Looks like you've come to stay for a while," he observed, pulling two of the heavily packed cases to the ground.

"I've come to stay permanently," she said, not realizing there was a brittle quality to her words.

"You couldn't make a smarter move," he told her.

Madeline frowned as she followed him toward the white two-storied house. She wondered how much her mother had told this man about her. Did he know she was divorced? Did he know the reason why? She cringed at the possibility.

"Why do you say that?"

They crossed the wide porch and Jake Hunter set the cases on the floor as he waited for her to open the door.

"Why, because of the city, of course. It's a charming, beautiful step back into history."

She breathed a bit easier. "Have you been here long, Mr. Hunter?"

"Since the first of the year. But call me Jake. It would sound ridiculous for your mother to call me Jake while you called me Mr. Hunter."

He followed her up the wide spiral staircase as though he was very familiar with the house. She wondered how well her mother knew this man. Was he merely a tenant who paid her a rent check each month, or were they actually friends?

She opened a door to the room that had always been hers. It was just off the wide second-floor balcony, and her heart lifted a bit when she saw the drapes drawn back from the French doors. The white balustrade gleamed in the sunshine, and just to the left a huge cypress tree draped with Spanish moss whispered against the railing.

Jake set the suitcases down by the bed and watched as Madeline lovingly trailed her fingers along the huge four-poster. A strange stirring hit him at the sad, almost regretful look on her face. He wondered who or what had put it there. The man she had divorced, or a lover, perhaps? He found both choices strangely distasteful.

"Don't bother with the last two. I can get them later," she assured him.

He waved away her words. "They're too heavy. I'll get them for you."

She started to protest but he vanished out the door. Sighing, she walked to the French doors and leaned against the framework. She could see a part of the backyard below.

Azaleas were in riotous bloom, the bushes covered with soft lilac, bright pink and white blossoms.

The Ozarks of Missouri had been beautiful, but this was where she had been born and raised; this was her life. This house had been built in the mid 1800s and had been passed down from generation to generation until it was now her mother's. It was in the middle of the historic district of Natchitoches, a place that in many ways had changed little since the days prior to the Civil War. This city, in fact, was the very first permanent settlement in the Louisiana Purchase. And that very permanence was the thing Madeline needed now. She needed to know that there were things in life that remained, that kept going no matter what, things that didn't end as her marriage to Andrew had.

"Here are the last two. I'll leave you to get settled in."

Jake Hunter's voice penetrated her thoughts and she turned to look at him.

"Thank you." She smiled at him. "You're very kind."

"Not always," he said with a grin and headed toward the door. "See you later."

Once Jake Hunter had disappeared, Madeline set about unpacking a couple of her suitcases. She did it methodically, unconsciously putting things in the same places she had stored them years ago.

She had not envisioned her return to Natchitoches quite the way it had actually happened. She had foreseen herself arriving alone and unnoticed, consumed with thoughts of finally leaving Ozark and Andrew behind her once and for all. But instead, she had found herself confronted with a frustrating, insistent man named Jake Hunter, and for a while all her disappointing memories had actually been forgotten.

She wished her mother would hurry up and get home. She wanted to ask Celia just why she had taken on a renter and what Jake Hunter was doing living in their backyard.

Deciding to leave the remaining suitcases for later, Madeline took a quick shower and put on a yellow flowered sundress. It showed off her slim waist and full breasts, and the skirt brushed sensuously against her long, slim legs when she walked.

Her copper-colored hair was nearly straight. When she took the pins from it and began to brush it, it fell from a side part and curved gently upon her shoulders.

Madeline had never considered herself a glamorous person, especially after she married Andrew. He was staid and conservative, not at all inclined to glamour of any sort, and he had never encouraged Madeline to play up her beauty in any way. It had taken her years to realize that he had subtly dominated her. Perhaps it was only now, after having spent a year away from him, that she could look back on their marriage and view it as it really had been.

She looked at the image in the mirror of her dressing table and smiled faintly. No, Andrew wouldn't approve of the way she looked now. He would think her dress too flamboyant, her hair too untidy, her makeup a bit overdone.

Well, Andrew, she thought while taking a deep breath, you're not a part of my life anymore. You can't tell me what to do or how to dress, and you can't keep reminding me just what a failure as a woman I am. Our divorce may have shaken my self-confidence, but I'll survive in spite of everything.

Laying the hairbrush aside, she walked to the French doors and opened them. The balcony had always been one of her favorite places, and even though it was hot outside, she left the air-conditioned comfort of her bedroom to lean against one of the white pillars.

She looked down at the old brick cabin that had been renovated into a guest house. It was partially shaded by a huge magnolia tree. There was another magnolia at the north end of the balcony. Both trees were over a hundred years old, and their branches were now so huge that they actually met to make a dark green canopy that reached from the main house to the guest house.

She was admiring the foliage when a flash of movement caught her eye. Turning her head slightly, she saw Jake Hunter leave the cabin and take a seat in one of the lawn chairs that were grouped together in the shade.

He was holding a glass. Probably whiskey, she thought. A cigarette was dangling from his lips and he held a book under his arm. He had changed shirts. The plaid one was gone and in its place was one with blue and white stripes. The sleeves were rolled up to his elbows.

He seemed very relaxed and contented as he smoked and read and sipped from his glass. For several minutes she watched him, knowing that he was unaware of her presence.

Apparently he was not married. She had been almost certain of that when he had pulled up to her on that monstrous-looking motorcycle. He did not appear to be a man who was tied to anyone or anything: he was obviously someone who enjoyed doing just as he pleased.

He was very different from Andrew in every way, and she had to admit that he intrigued her. It was probably this difference that had made her curious, she realized. The men she had been around the past few years were not the type who said and did just what they felt; they all led very conventional, predictable lives.

Madeline wondered how long Jake Hunter was planning to stay in Natchitoches and then reminded herself that the answer to that question had nothing to do with her. She had no intention of ever becoming involved with a man again. Andrew and the pain of the last few years had been enough to teach her the hazards of the heart.

"Madeline? Are you in there, honey?"

At the sound of her mother's voice, Madeline quickly left the balcony and hurried through the bedroom.

Celia poked her head around the door, but when she saw Madeline she rushed into the room and flung her arms around her daughter.

"Oh, darling!" she exclaimed. "It's so wonderful to have you back home. Let me look at you!"

After a moment she took a step away from Madeline and said, "Well, you certainly don't have the look of a depressed woman who's just gone through a divorce."

Madeline smiled faintly. "I take it that's a compliment?"

"It definitely is!" Celia stated, grinning enthusiastically. "Much longer with Andrew and you'd have become the perfect frump."

Surprised, Madeline gasped. "Mother! You never hinted that I looked dowdy before."

Celia, who had always been one to keep up with fashion, clucked her tongue. "Madeline, you never looked dowdy. Subdued, maybe, but not dowdy." She laughed and squeezed Madeline's hand. "This is the way you should look, the way you used to look seven years ago, when you were twenty-one and working at Maria's dress shop, remember?"

Madeline laughed as the two women linked arms and started down the staircase to the main living area of the house.

"Yes, I do remember. So much has happened since then. But I still want that dress shop, now more than ever."

"You don't know how happy that makes me," Celia said and sighed. "For a while there I was so worried about you. I knew you were depressed, but I also knew you were going to have to work your own way out of it. You know, when your father and I divorced it was traumatic for me. You were still a teenager and I had that paltry job at the newspaper office."

Madeline nodded somberly at the memory. It had not been a happy time for any of them.

Celia smiled at her daughter as if to tell her not to dwell on the past. "You'll make it, darling. You've enough of me in you to make sure you keep fighting."

What had once been an elegant drawing room had been refurbished by Celia into a relaxed den area. It was filled with modern furniture covered with navy-blue and yellow prints. The wall hangings and many of the other pieces in the room were bright and beautiful.

"Would you like a drink before dinner?" Celia asked.

Madeline shook her head. "I don't think so."

"Oh, come on," she insisted. "One cocktail won't hurt you. I'll make it a weak one."

"Very well," Madeline agreed, watching her mother walk to the wet bar. At forty-eight, Celia looked much younger than her years. Her hair was blond, not quite as thick as Madeline's, and she wore it in a short, casual style. She was tall and still willowy. Madeline realized she may have gotten her red hair from her father's side of the family but she had definitely inherited her mother's figure, something for which she would be eternally thankful.

"Are we going out for dinner?" Madeline asked as her mother pressed a glass into her hand.

"I thought about it, but then I was afraid you'd be exhausted from the drive. So I brought home a box of crawfish."

"Mmm, wonderful," Madeline said. It had been a long time since she'd had any good, boiled, Louisiana crawfish. Her mother was always so thoughtful.

"By the way, have you run into Jake yet?" Celia sipped her drink and plopped down in an armchair opposite Madeline.

"Jake Hunter, the man renting the guest cabin," Madeline said. "Yes, I've met him. I couldn't believe you neglected to tell me about taking on a tenant!"

Celia smiled vaguely. "I know you, Maddie. And if I had told you a man was staying here you would never have agreed to come back home."

Madeline crossed her legs and tapped the air nervously with the toe of her white flat. "You're probably right," she conceded. "Men are not exactly my favorite things in the world right now. But that's beside the point. Whether you rent the guest house or not is your business. Besides," she added, surprising herself somewhat, "Jake Hunter seems nice enough; I don't think he and I will have any run-ins."

"I'm so glad to see you don't mind his being here," her mother said happily, then put her drink aside and rose to her feet. "Right now, I think I'll go change out of these work clothes, and then we'll carry our dinner out back. How does that sound?"

"Lovely," Madeline said. She watched her mother leave the room, and then suddenly remembered. "By the way, Mom, what does Jake Hunter do for a living?"

Celia turned slightly as she reached the doorway. "Oh, I forgot to mention it. Jake's a writer. Novels."

Madeline's brows lifted in disbelief. "A writer? I don't recall seeing anything in the bookstores by a Jake Hunter. Has he had anything published?"

Celia laughed as though Madeline's question was absolutely ridiculous. "I'd say he's had quite a few sales. Jake is Harlon Howard."

Madeline stared at her mother in absolute horror, but Celia seemed not to notice the distress in her daughter's face. She was already heading toward the staircase. "By the way, I forgot to mention that I've invited Jake to share supper with us. I hope you don't mind. He's all alone, you know. And he's such a dear."

Before Madeline had a chance to protest, her mother was already out of sight. Madeline took a rather large swallow of the Tom Collins and stared disbelievingly into space.

Harlon Howard! This was incredible! The man who had offered to give her a ride on a motorcycle, the man who had lain on the floorboard of her car, the man to whom she had been so blatantly cool, had been Harlon Howard!

She took another sip of the Tom Collins and felt her cheeks grow hot with mortification. She had even suspected him of being a thief!

Putting the drink aside, Madeline began to move restlessly around the room. Could she face Jake Hunter over supper? Their exchange on the street made it embarrassing enough, but now her mind was consumed with the idea that Jake was the man who had written all those steamy southern blockbusters.

Andrew had called his writing nothing but pulp. He had said that Harlon Howard was a man making an outrageous living by writing erotic stories and that he had no literary talent to speak of. Madeline had always disagreed. She had even read three Harlon Howard novels. True, she had found them to be sexually explicit, but there had been far more than sex to his books. His vivid descriptions of historical periods were extraordinarily accurate, or at least seemed to be to Madeline. Also, his stark use of words made the characters seem so real that she had found it nearly impossible to put one of Harlon Howard's books down for any length of time.

At that moment she heard Celia coming down the stairs. Madeline turned to see that her mother had changed into a pair of red pedal pushers and a white over blouse. Madeline left the drawing room to join her.

"I made some coleslaw this morning before I left for work so all we need to do is get plates and silverware."

Celia crossed the spacious kitchen and pulled the bowl of coleslaw from the fridge. Madeline opened the cabinets and began to take down stoneware plates.

"What are we drinking? Shall I get glasses or coffee cups?" Madeline asked.

Celia glanced over her shoulder. "Get the wine goblets from the china cabinet."

"Wine goblets! Mother, we just had a drink. What are you trying to do to me? Stone me out of my depression?" She said it half-jokingly but wondered if maybe that actually was her mother's intention. After all, Celia had always thought her daughter too unbending.

Celia laughed. "Maddie, darling, your humor is so dry at times. We are merely having wine because Jake kindly offered to supply it for our meal."

Madeline sighed and started toward the dining room in search of the goblets. She couldn't believe her first night back home was going to be spent with a famous writer and a bottle of wine. It was the very last thing she had expected. And it was, she was certain, the very last thing she needed.

Chapter Two

There was a huge, screened porch attached to the back of the Beaumont house. Situated at one end of it was a round wicker table and several matching chairs.

Hanging baskets of pink and white impatiens swung from the rafters while ferns and palms gave one the feeling of stepping into a tropical garden. Madeline loved the way her mother had decorated the porch. It was soothing and restful, a place that invited a person to relax. But Madeline didn't really expect to relax tonight, in spite of her surroundings.

She was placing the silverware beside the plates when Jake appeared at the door of his cabin. He noticed her presence when he was halfway across the yard.

"Hello again, Madeline. Or did I ever say hello the first time?" he asked while stepping onto the porch.

Madeline waited until the screen door shut behind him before she said, "No, I don't believe you did." It was more like, Hop on my motorcycle, baby, and I'll give you a ride, she thought, even if he hadn't actually said those words.

He handed Madeline the bottle of wine, which she noticed was of a very expensive vintage. Without comment she placed it in the center of the table.

"I hope you don't mind sharing your first evening home with me. Celia has spoken so much of you that I feel like I'm welcoming home an old friend."

His words were very warmly spoken, and she believed he was sincere. However, a chill rushed through her in spite of his attitude.

Celia has spoken so much of you, she repeated to herself. Just what had her mother told this man? If she had told him anything personal, Madeline would want to choke her!

"Mothers are biased. You shouldn't believe half of what she says about me."

Jake chuckled and took a seat in a yellow-cushioned lawn chair at the other end of the porch. She watched as he leaned back and stretched his arms behind his head.

He had a lazy, catlike sensuality that irritated Madeline. It had irritated her from the very first time she had seen him. In spite of everything she had been through, it reminded her that she was still a woman with emotions and desires: something she had tried desperately to forget.

"Don't worry, your mother hasn't divulged all your deep, dark secrets," he said, a crooked grin on his face.

Madeline knew he was teasing, yet she turned her eyes from him. She had a feeling that Jake Hunter was a man who could see right through a person, a man from whom it would be difficult to keep anything hidden.

Madeline forced herself to smile as she fussed unnecessarily with the table napkins. "What makes you think I have any deep, dark secrets?"

Jake chuckled once again. "Because everyone does, don't they?"

"I suppose these days it's unfashionable not to," Madeline answered evasively. She turned and faced him, her back resting lightly against the table edge. "So, how do you like living in Natchitoches?" she asked, deliberately changing the subject.

"I've really enjoyed it so far," he said. "Natchitoches has such an enormous amount of history that I'm always discovering interesting things. And, of course, your mother has made it doubly pleasant by letting me lease the guest house."

Madeline pushed away from the table and took the chair opposite him. She wished her mother would hurry up. It made her edgy to be out here alone with this man. She didn't really know why. She only knew that when she looked at him, she couldn't help but recall all those steamy passages he had written. The knowledge that those erotic scenes had been created by this man made her intensely uncomfortable. She tried to push it out of her mind as she said, "I haven't learned exactly how you came to rent from Mother. Did she have the cabin advertised?"

Jake shook his head, making Madeline notice his hair. It was a beautiful color, that shade of brown that stops just short of being black, but still has the warmth of rich, dark coffee. It fell from a side part and covered most of his forehead. At first glance it looked straight, but on closer inspection she could see it curled slightly at the ends.

"I happened to be in the bank, opening an account, and Celia overheard me say I was hunting for a place," he told her. "She kindly offered me the guest house and I snatched it up. It's hard to find nice, private places for any length of time, and I detest living in hotels, which is what I was doing when I met your mother. No matter what you do, you can never make them home."

And he considered the guest house his home? Was he planning to stay that long? She didn't want to dwell on that possibility. "And where is your home—your real home, I mean?"

He seemed to be looking at her face, but she was sure he was also taking in the scooped neckline of her dress and the emerald pendant that insisted on nestling in the shallow cleft between her breasts.

"I have a house in Atlanta and an apartment in New York City. But I like to think that home is where I happen to be at the time. And as for now, Natchitoches is my home."

Hearing footsteps, Madeline hurriedly rose to her feet and opened the screen door for her mother. She was carrying a tray loaded with boiled crawfish, coleslaw and hot buttered rolls.

Madeline quickly took the tray from her mother and carried it to the table. Meanwhile Jake rose to his feet and eyed Celia with obvious amusement.

"Celia, you really didn't have to dress for my benefit," he said dryly.

Celia looked down at her red pedal pushers in mock offense. "Well, I had so much trouble deciding between my lamé gown and the black silk that I finally decided on this."

"Perfect choice," Jake assured her, winking charmingly as he followed Celia to the table. "I'm glad I put my black tails back in the closet."

Celia laughed and Madeline glanced at her mother and Jake Hunter. Their friendly bantering sparked an emotion inside her that she couldn't quite describe. It wasn't jealousy. It couldn't be. Still, as they all took their seats around the table, she felt a faint sadness, an isolation as she listened to them joke with each other.

There had never been anyone in Madeline's life with whom she could share such casual, relaxing moments. No one with whom she could let her hair down, act silly if she wanted and not be afraid of getting put down for it.

She remembered the early years of her marriage, back when she had still been like her mother, full of zest and life and a natural love of people.

Since Andrew had been a stockbroker they had often had to attend parties of one sort or another. After these parties Madeline had grown to expect scathing chastisements from her husband. According to him, she had always been too talkative or, even worse, flirtatious. In an attempt to keep the peace between them, Madeline had finally subdued her bubbly personality and become the sedate wife Andrew wanted.

Now as she listened to Celia and Jake, resentment welled up within her. She hated herself for allowing a man to change her so completely, to deprive her of so many things. She was determined more than ever never to let it happen again.

Madeline came out of her reverie as Jake pulled the cork from the wine bottle. He filled Celia's glass, then Madeline's and finally his own.

His hands were large and strong-looking, their backs sprinkled with dark brown hair. They did not look like hands that pounded a typewriter, Madeline found herself thinking, but more like hands that spent their time sliding over a woman's skin.

Madeline's thoughts came to an abrupt halt. What was the matter with her? Why did these wild notions keep running through her mind? They had to stop!

"Celia, you didn't tell me Maddie was a redhead who could wear yellow better than a canary," Jake said, bringing an embarrassed tinge of color to Madeline's cheeks.

Celia laughed and looked lovingly at her daughter. "I guess you can see for yourself that Madeline didn't get her looks from me. She's a Beaumont through and through: red hair, green eyes. But believe me, she has my heart. Don't you, darling?"

Smiling faintly, Madeline nodded while Jake studied her over the rim of his wineglass. It was hard for him to believe that this quiet, somewhat aloof woman was even remotely related to Celia. He wondered if she was always this staid, or if she was reacting this way only because he was present.

"My Fiat broke down before I made it home," Madeline informed her mother. "Jake happened to come along and fix it for me."

Celia arched her eyebrows in surprise. "Really? Where were you?"

"Near the Fort Claiborne house. At least it didn't happen farther back."

Celia laughed lightly. "I can't imagine you trusting Jake enough to let him look at your car."

"Actually, I thought he was a car thief," she said, suddenly deciding to be truthful.

Jake laughed deeply. The sound of his laughter reminded Madeline of warm, flowing honey.

"Believe me, Celia, I had to bully her. Is she always so stubborn?"

Celia smiled. "She doesn't have red hair for nothing. But Asa always was stubborn, too. She comes by it naturally. By the way, Maddie, I heard from your father at Easter."

Madeline was surprised, to say the least. They had rarely heard from Asa Beaumont since he left them so many years before. But strangely enough neither Madeline nor Celia felt bitter toward him. Asa was a man who should never have married in the first place. He had wanderlust in his veins and his job as a merchant marine had always been the most important thing in his life. Celia had realized that early in their marriage, and Madeline had gradually come to understand it as she had grown older. Still, in spite of all the years without him, she still loved her father.

"I hope he was doing well," she said.

"They had just put in port somewhere in the Caribbean. He was going to spend Easter lying under a palm, drinking rum and soda."

Jake laughed and Madeline smiled.

"Not exactly a bad way to be spending the holiday," Jake said. "Palms, warm sand, the sea—I'd say he was doing quite well."

"Do you like to sail?" Madeline asked, passing him the bowl of coleslaw.

"For a couple of days, then I like to put solid ground beneath my feet again."

Madeline broke one of the red crawfish and tasted the delicious meat. "Mmm, this is exactly what I've been needing."

Jake cracked the tail on his own crawfish, grinning wryly. "Your mother had her work cut out for her to get me to try these things. Now I'm addicted. New England may have lobsters, but Louisiana has the crawfish."

"I've introduced Jake to quite a few Cajun dishes," Celia announced. "And since he's here to research his next novel, it gave me a good excuse for cooking and eating."

Madeline's eyes turned to Jake once again. She still felt oddly threatened by him, even though she was struggling not to. "Oh, is the novel going to be set in this area?"

He nodded. "Right here on the banks of the Cane River. I plan to do a saga, beginning with the arrival of St. Denis and his bold romance with Emanuelle Sanchez de Navarro and continuing on through the Civil War."

"That sounds like a major project," Madeline said. "You're covering lots of years."

He grinned slyly. "That's what makes it interesting and challenging."

Madeline would have liked to ask him many things about his writing, but didn't. She was sure that as soon as people found out who he was, he was constantly plagued with annoying questions. Since Madeline was a very private person herself, she treated other people in the same manner.

It was well after dark by the time they'd eaten the last crawfish. The night was warm and muggy, and they sat out under the magnolias and cypress trees to drink their coffee.

After a while Jake went to his cabin door and let out a fat gray tabby cat whom he called Mr. Miles. The cat devoured the scraps from the crawfish as though he hadn't seen a meal in weeks.

"Why do you call him Mr. Miles?" Madeline asked, thinking the animal would never win a cat show. One ear looked as though it had been chewed at one time or another and the tip of his tail had surely been broken. He couldn't have been born with one that crooked.

Jake shrugged and tossed the tomcat a piece of roll he had been eating with his coffee. Unbelievably, the cat ate the bread, too. "I found him on a street in New York City. It was raining and he was wet and bedraggled. It looked as though he had walked for miles and still hadn't found a home."

"So Jake nobly gave him one," Celia told her daughter.

"Well," Jake said rather modestly, "Mr. Miles may not have a permanent address but he goes wherever I go and that's good enough for him."

Mr. Miles seemed to know they were discussing him. He rubbed against Jake's jean-clad leg and then pranced over to Madeline and jumped straight into her lap.

Madeline was surprised at the instant trust the cat placed in her, and scratched him fondly between the ears.

Jake watched them both, an amused expression on his face. "I think Mr. Miles once belonged to a woman. He likes practically all females. He only tolerates me because I feed and shelter him."

"It's his pride," Madeline replied. "He doesn't like sharing his territory with another male."

"Humph," Jake snorted, arching an eyebrow menacingly at the cat. "You might just sleep outside tonight, Mr. Miles."

Celia laughed at that, but Madeline didn't find it amusing. She patted the tomcat's head and assured him he could sleep with her if Jake should make good on his threat.

Jake muttered something about ruining the cat for life just as Celia got up to refill their coffee cups. Madeline's cheeks had colored at Jake's suggestive remark, and she hoped her mother wouldn't notice. Knowing Celia, she would read all kinds of things into it.

"Oh, I just remembered, Maddie. There's a place on Front Street that's going to be up for lease soon."

Madeline was suddenly all ears. This news was too good to be true. She had always dreamed of having a dress shop there. Everyone who visited Natchitoches invariably made a trip down Front Street. Cane River Lake ran through the city like a highway of water. The street ran adjacent to it and had a beautiful view. Front Street was also the focal point of the city's festivals and yearly gatherings and the perfect place for Madeline to open her business. "That's hard to believe. When did you hear this news?"

"Just today. The law firm that has the second floor of one of the buildings is moving over near the modern shopping centers."

"I wonder if they've already rented it," Madeline said thoughtfully. "With my luck, probably. Besides, do you think an upstairs shop would work?"

"If you make it inviting enough," Jake interjected. "A climb up a staircase won't daunt women when it comes to buying clothes. Especially if they're fashionable and priced right."

He seemed awfully sure of what he was saying. Did the man think he knew that much about women? Stupid question, Madeline thought. From the way he wrote about women, he knew them inside and out.

"Jake is right, Maddie. So why don't you go take a look at it?" Celia suggested. "I'm sure Jake would drive you around."

Madeline's green eyes widened as she stared at her mother. There was no way she would let Celia start match-making. She might as well make that clear right now. "I don't think that will be necessary. I do know how to drive, and I'm sure looking at a building for a future dress shop is not exactly Jake's idea of enjoyment."

Celia looked sheepish and just a little angry. Jake's face was expressionless as he set his coffee on a low table near his lawn chair. It was impossible for Madeline to tell what he was thinking.

"How do you know that, Maddie?" he inquired. "For your information, I like any reason to go down to Front Street."

He rose to his feet and signaled to the gray tomcat. "Miles, down. I'm taking the lady for a ride."

Amazingly, as if he were in cahoots with his master, the cat obeyed and jumped gracefully from Madeline's lap.

"I don't—it's unnecessary to go now. Besides, it's dark. We couldn't really see anything."

"There are streetlights," Jake said simply.

"Don't be silly, Maddie, I'm sure you're dying to see it," her mother insisted.

Madeline reluctantly rose to her feet and brushed the wrinkles from her skirt. It would be ridiculous to continue making flimsy excuses. After all, Jake was merely being friendly; it was her own reluctance that was posing the problem.

"Yes, I would like to see it, even though it will probably be a while before I can get any real capital to put into the place."

"Good, you two go on then, and I'll clean our dinner mess away," Celia said happily, already starting to gather up the coffee cups.

Madeline followed Jake to the driveway and waited while he fished a key from his pocket. When he started toward the black motorcycle, Madeline stared at him in disbelief.

"You don't expect me to ride that thing, do you?" she demanded.

Undaunted, he grinned at her, and Madeline knew that here was a man so different than her ex-husband they could have been from opposite ends of the earth. Andrew would have died if she had even thought of riding a motorcycle, much less actually done it.

"Surely you're not afraid," he said. "Haven't you ever ridden a motorcycle?"

Madeline nodded as he straddled the big machine and kicked back the kickstand with his brown roper boot.

"Years ago when I was a teenager," she said. "In fact, I thought these things were only for teenagers."

He chuckled mockingly as he stared at her. "And you think you have to quit doing certain things just because you get older? That seems to me to be a pretty boring outlook on life."

Madeline couldn't see this man forcing himself to do anything that bored him. But then, why should he? she wondered. He was independently wealthy, his own boss and, as far as she knew, he had to account to no one. How that must feel!

Then suddenly Madeline realized that she had no one to account to any longer, either. After a moment's hesitation she decided, what the heck. Very carefully she straddled the seat behind him and tucked her flowered skirt safely beneath her legs.

She tried not to think of the pleased look on Jake's face as he started backing out the driveway. It was more than pleased; it was triumphant.

"Hold on to my waist, Maddie," he instructed before he put the bike into motion.

Self-consciously Madeline placed both hands at the side of his waist only to have him say, "No, not like that! Put your arms around me and hold tight. I won't accuse you of taking liberties."

Her green eyes rolled heavenward as she did his bidding. The man was ... she couldn't think of a word. Somewhere between insufferable and charming. Maybe exciting was the way to describe him, for she did have to admit holding on to his lean, hard waist as they ripped through the street was exciting.

Front Street was only a few short blocks away, and Jake slowed down when they approached the river. As they traveled alongside it a ski boat passed with happy, laughing people aboard. Jake pointed it out to Madeline.

She nodded in acknowledgment, wishing she were on the boat and wondering what it must be like to do such enjoyable things. Andrew had never been an athletic person so the few activities they had shared usually involved such indoor events as movies or a night at the symphony. Those things were fine, but Madeline had frequently longed for more simple, relaxed outings, even if it had merely meant sitting under a tree in a park and sharing a soft drink.

The idea made Madeline laugh ruefully. Andrew sitting under a tree was unimaginable; he couldn't afford to stain his slacks, and blue jeans were never part of his wardrobe.

Jake parked the motorcycle not far from the bridge that crossed the river to join St. Clair Avenue. Even though it was dark, a few people were still about on the streets and down by the river. Madeline soaked in the sights. She had grown up here, and she felt an overwhelming sense of homecoming at this moment.

"Sort of sets you back in time, doesn't it?"

Jake's voice stirred Madeline from her thoughts, and she looked away from the river and brushed back her wind-blown hair.

"Yes, very much so." She smiled faintly at him. "In more ways than one."

He was gazing out over the river. "Every time I drive down this street I get the urge to run back home and scratch down a few more lines. It's so easy to picture this place in the 1800s: the horse-drawn buggies, the women in hoop-skirts, the barbecues out under the oaks and cypresses, the southern chivalry. We'll never see the likes of them again."

"But we can read about them, thanks to writers like you."

He looked at her, his gray eyes narrowed, a smile on his face. "Hmm, is that a compliment?"

She shrugged and turned away from the river so that she could see the French-styled buildings in front of them. "I suppose it is." She didn't want to sound too flowery. He didn't need compliments; he knew he was a success. She wondered what kind of feeling that was.

Instinctively they crossed the street and then strolled beneath the awnings of the buildings. Since the street was not very long, it was simple to find the law offices her mother had told them about. Madeline studied the structure for a long time, craning her neck to look at its front. It was difficult trying to imagine herself working in the confines of this small building.

"Well, the front looks nice enough," Jake commented. "Of course you can't really tell anything until you see the inside."

"Yes," she agreed. "Perhaps they'll be vacating soon. I think I'll call tomorrow and get all the information. The rent may be more than I can manage."

"It's an old building. Surely they couldn't ask an arm and a leg for it?"

"But that's just it, Jake. Because it is old and here in the historic district, I'm afraid they *will* be asking an arm and a leg for it."

Madeline didn't realize how easily his name came from her lips until after she had spoken it.

She found herself suddenly looking up into his eyes, and from the faint gleam in them she knew he had not missed her use of his name. As Madeline gazed back at him she thought his eyes were rather beautiful in the darkness, silvery and enchanting like the moon against a black sky.

"Does this dress shop mean that much to you?" he asked quietly.

Madeline thought for a moment because now that she was actually confronted with the question she wasn't quite sure.

"Not the dress shop itself," she answered truthfully. "But just making a success at it, I suppose. I know that must seem small-scale to you, but to me it's like a baby taking its first steps."

He frowned as though her words disappointed him. "Believe me, Maddie, being successful is not what it's all about. Being happy along the way is."

She sighed and turned away from the building, her eyes filled with a sad torment as she stared across the river to the other side of the city. He couldn't know how she felt. He couldn't know that she had failed at everything she had set out to do in life. Her failure had left her with an empty, hollow feeling and she was at a loss as to how to fill her life once again. She sometimes doubted she could.

"That's easy for you to say," she murmured. "I can't imagine how you feel. You must live on a constant high."

He laughed and it was just as warm and pleasant-sounding to Madeline as it had been earlier.

"Hardly. I may be a successful writer, but that doesn't mean I've always had what I wanted. I've learned in my thirty-eight years of living that success is just the end result of doing something that makes you happy." With an impish smile he reached out and tugged at a few strands of her red hair. "Of course the money doesn't hurt."

"Yes, I'm sure." Madeline laughed softly, trying not to think about his fingers in her hair. How long had it been since a man had touched her hair? She couldn't remember when Andrew had last touched it.

Jake moved a step closer, and Madeline's heart began to pound. It was a frightening sensation, for she had never known her heart to react to anything in such a rapid, violent way.

She moved away from him, hoping the distance would calm the scary pounding within her.

"Why are you afraid of me, Maddie?" he questioned softly. "Is it just because I'm a man, or because you've learned that I'm Harlon Howard?"

She studied his face in the darkness. She could hear a motorboat down on the river and a car moving slowly along the street, but the sounds hardly registered. As she looked into Jake's eyes she was shocked to discover that she didn't think of him merely as a man or as Harlon Howard, the successful novelist. She thought of him only as Jake, and she wondered what it would be like to be Jake's woman.

"Neither idea frightens me," she told him in a quick, breathy voice. God, how far her thoughts about this man had come in just a few hours! What was she going to be thinking tomorrow and the next day?

He seemed to know that she was lying, at least partially. She watched him inspect the strands of her coppery hair between his fingers. The color was vibrant against his tanned skin. She wondered what it would look like against his bare chest, then swallowed convulsively at the image forming in her mind.

"Your ex-husband must have been insane to let a woman like you go," he said, his voice so low she almost couldn't hear him. "I don't think I'd be quite as stupid."

Madeline could not believe he was saying these things to her, especially here in the dark on a public street. "A woman like me?" she asked bitterly. "You have no idea what kind of woman I am."

He took hold of her hand and led her back across the brick street to the motorcycle. "I'm perfectly willing to let you show me."

Madeline barely grasped his words. She was too busy thinking about the touch of his hand against hers. She found the sensation was so pleasant it actually terrified her.

Chapter Three

Since the night is so beautiful, why don't we walk down by the river?" he suggested, once they were back at his Harley-Davidson.

Madeline hesitated before answering. Spending more time with this man than she had to would be asking for problems. Coming back home to Natchitoches was supposed to help her get her life back into perspective again. How could she do that when she was becoming obsessed with a man she had met only hours before?

"Isn't it getting late? Mother might worry about us," she said.

She could tell by the look on his face how ludicrous he thought her excuse sounded. "Maddie, we're only a few blocks away. If she gets that worried she'll come look for us herself."

Madeline took a deep breath and then nodded weakly. This had been a strange day anyway. Why not go along with the rest of it, she decided.

"Well, it is a beautiful night," she agreed.

He took her by the arm, and they started down the steep, sloping riverbank. A paved street ran along the side of the river, and at intervals there were boat ramps. Jake and Madeline decided to stroll on the grass a few feet away from the water's edge.

Every now and then Jake casually touched the small of her back and Madeline had a hard time keeping her mind off his touch and on his words. She tried to remember back when she had started dating and how she had reacted to a man's touch then. It had not been like this. There had not been the intense, searing reaction she had to Jake Hunter. She had to overcome it or she was headed for deep trouble.

"You sound Georgian. Is that where you're from originally?" she asked.

He nodded. "I lived in New York City for a few years, and I still keep an apartment there, but I guess even that didn't affect my accent much."

"You—you have a family there—in Georgia, I mean?"

"My dad and a younger sister. My mother died a couple of years back."

"Do you see them often?" she asked curiously.

"Not as often as I should. Dad's still deeply involved in his textile business and Loretta has a big family to manage. But when I'm home and not out roaming and researching we do have our times together."

"Mmm, must be nice," she said, her voice wistful. "It's only Mother and me, so I've always missed that family feeling. But I guess I'm lucky to have her."

He chuckled softly. "Celia has been a delight to know. She can be very amusing at times. And very independent."

Madeline nodded. "She's had to be. My father left when I was only fourteen. She's been on her own ever since."

"Well, if I know Celia, the idea of making it on her own didn't scare her half as much as it did me when I was trying to make my mark in the world as a writer."

Surprised by his words, she glanced at him. "You've been a success for a long time. Your first book, *Bitter Harvest*, was a bestseller and that was years ago. It must not have taken you long to make your mark."

He seemed more impressed that she remembered his first novel than by what she had said as a whole. "So you remember *Bitter Harvest*. I was very immature when I wrote that. I look back on it and wonder how it ever became successful."

"The action and the shocking twists of the plot, I would say. At least, that's why I liked it."

He looked at her quizzically. He hadn't thought she was the type to read novels, at least not novels of his kind. *Bitter Harvest* was a postdepression era book, set in the south. It had dealt with poverty, ignorance, bigotry, greed and even murder. He could not imagine this woman reading and liking it. He told himself he still had a lot to learn about women and about writing. "So you read?"

"Yes. I can actually spell and do calculations, too."

It was the first time he had heard her come close to joking, and for a moment it took him by surprise. Then he chuckled and said, "I'm glad to know there's a little humor in you somewhere. For a while I thought you were one of those how-can-I-laugh-when-there's-dying-all-around-me kind of people."

Madeline shook her head, a faint smile on her lips. "Maybe I should work harder on my image. I won't be able to sell anything if that's the kind of signal I'm giving off."

His hand was suddenly on her arm. She stopped to look at him questioningly. A muggy little breeze blew off the river and played with the dark hair that fell across his forehead. She wondered how many women he had been involved with in the past. If his looks were anything to go on, probably far too many.

"I'd like to help you change that image," he said softly.

Madeline's eyes met his. He was studying her with an expectancy that surprised her. But a soft little smile curved his lips. It said, Trust me, I won't hurt you. Right at that moment Madeline wanted to believe that smile and everything it promised.

"How?"

His fingers tightened on her arm as she whispered the question. At the back of her head his other hand tangled in the silken red strands of her hair.

Madeline stood as if hypnotized upon the riverbank. Her legs began to tremble and that illogical pounding of her heart started again. She had never felt so defenseless in her life.

When his mouth settled over hers, Madeline involuntarily shuddered, and her fingers clutched at his shirt. She was certain that the ground beneath them had suddenly joined the river and they were being pulled away by the current.

His lips were hard and warm and tasted distinctly masculine. He was kissing her hungrily and—unbelievably—she was matching that hunger. When his tongue slid into the sweet cavity of her mouth she felt as though she were only one breath away from actually making love with this man. She hadn't known, in spite of her marriage to Andrew, that a kiss could be so all-consuming, that it could cause a sweet, insidious ache to grow within her. An ache so overwhelming that she actually whimpered against his lips and pressed herself ever closer to his hard body.

Her mind kept repeating that here was the man who could ease the passionate ache of her body, as well as the ache in her heart.

Sometime during the embrace his hands had moved to her breasts. "God, Maddie!" he whispered hoarsely. "We're out here in the open, but all I can think about is getting you out of this dress and onto the ground."

The little time it took him to speak was enough to let sanity come crashing back to Madeline. She couldn't believe she had become so totally oblivious to everything while in this man's arms! The idea terrified her and she jerked away from him and began running up the steep slope of the river.

"Madeline! Come back!"

She heard his voice but did not heed his words. Tears of shock and humiliation streamed down her face, and she wished she had the strength to run forever, to run so fast and so hard that neither Jake Hunter nor any man could ever reach her.

By the time the chamber of commerce building loomed before her she was fighting for breath. She leaned against its brick walls just behind a clump of flowering shrubs. Maybe Jake would be so angry with her he would go home and leave her alone. She hoped he would! She felt as if she could never look him in the face again, as if she could never trust herself to be near him again!

"Madeline?"

It was Jake's voice and she stared into the darkness, desperately wiping the tears from her cheeks.

He spotted her even though she made no sound. He was breathing easily as though the run up the riverbank had been nothing for him. Madeline's breasts were still heaving from the effort.

"Madeline, why did you do that? Why did you run away?"

He put his hand under her chin, and as he lifted up her face the teardrops glistened on her cheeks like diamonds.

"Oh, Jake," she moaned. "Don't you know? I wanted to make love to you! I—I still do!"

His hands gently smoothed her hair and then curved around her shoulders. "Is that so bad?" he asked, thoroughly confused.

"Yes." She gasped. "I don't even know you. And thank God you don't know me!"

She was trembling. Jake calmly took her into his arms and let her bury her face against his chest. Madeline drank in the smell and touch of him while trying to figure out how it was possible to feel secure and threatened in his arms simultaneously.

"You don't know what you're saying, Madeline," he said softly. "I want to know you in every way a man can know a woman."

She gripped the front of his shirt and choked back a sob. "You'd only be disappointed," she told him. Suddenly she lifted her face up to his; her green eyes beseeched him to understand.

"I like you, Jake. I like you very much. Don't ask more from me."

His steady gaze took in her moist eyes, her trembling lips, the red flame of her hair. He realized he had never been more mesmerized.

"I won't make promises to you that I can't keep."

Madeline thought about his words all the way home and well into the night.

The next morning Celia Beaumont studied her daughter over the rim of her coffee cup. She didn't like the dark smudges beneath Madeline's eyes or her lethargic movements.

"So, are you going to call about the vacant space in that building?" Celia questioned, glancing at her watch.

Madeline pushed back her loose hair and took a bite of buttered biscuit. "Yes, I promise I'll call. But it may not do any good to get the lease if the house isn't sold in Ozark. I don't want to borrow that much money. In fact, the way the economy is, I doubt that I could. Small businesses are a bad risk right now, and I don't have any collateral."

"Andrew is working on the sale, isn't he? I mean, he's not dallying with the house in an effort to keep things dangling between you two?"

Madeline laughed bitterly. "Andrew is as anxious to sever all ties with me as I am with him. He's married again, you know. Two months ago."

Celia grimaced. "No. You didn't tell me. Who's the unlucky lady?"

Madeline shrugged and was happy to find that the thought of Andrew marrying again did not seem nearly as devastating as it had only a short time ago.

"Someone he met in the business. She's very young and can give him what he wants. He's already made sure of it."

"You mean . . . ?" Celia said, then broke off in amazement as Madeline nodded. "I always knew he was an ass. This just proves it even more."

Madeline couldn't agree more. The woman had been pregnant and Andrew, worried as ever about appearances and what people might think of him, rushed to marry her. Madeline just hoped that the poor woman would be happier with Andrew than she herself had ever been. Maybe the birth of the baby would change Andrew's personality for the better, she mused. After all he had desperately wanted a child for some time now.

"Oh, Maddie," her mother groaned. "When are you going to stop being down on yourself? When are you going to face the fact that nothing could have saved your marriage? Andrew was never the man for you. I knew it before you ever married him. You're lucky you're out of it."

Madeline reached for her coffee, hoping the caffeine would revive her. "Mother, I can't believe you, of all people, would be sitting there lauding divorce—your own daughter's divorce."

"Darling, I've been married," Celia defended herself. "I have just as much respect for the marriage vows as the next person. But not—I repeat, not—when I see one person destroying another. Andrew played on the goodness of your heart for years. He did his best to change you to what he wanted. It was always what he wanted no matter how much you suffered."

Shaking her head with conviction Celia got up from the kitchen table. "You're my daughter and I want you to be happy more than anything in my life. If the house doesn't sell soon, we'll work something else out. My job at the bank has to mean something."

This brought a smile to Madeline's lips. "You think you can throw your weight around a little?"

Celia laughed and crossed the room to pick up her handbag from the cabinet counter. "Working in the loans department might give me a little edge."

Madeline rose from the table to follow her mother to the door. "Okay, I'll make the call. I think I'll even go over and see Maria at her dress shop. If anyone can give me advice, she can."

Celia leaned over and kissed her daughter's cheek. "That's a lovely idea. I know she wants to see you again."

"Have a good day," Madeline said as her mother started down the steps.

"Oh, I almost forgot," Celia added. "Don't start supper. Jake is taking us out tonight."

"Jake!" Madeline stared at her mother in horror. "Why is he taking us out? Are we going to be sharing every meal with the man!"

Looking puzzled, Celia turned back to her daughter. "Maddie, what's wrong with you? You sound like a hysterical shrew this morning."

Madeline took a calming breath. Her cheeks were hot and she knew they were probably red. "Nothing is the matter," she lied. "I just—it would be nice to have some time alone with my mother."

Celia smiled with understanding. "Darling, we will, I promise. But I didn't want to disappoint Jake. He's such a sweet guy. And after all, he was our guest last night. He wants to return the favor."

Last night! Just what favor did he really want to return, Madeline wondered wildly. "Well, I guess one night won't hurt. Will we be dressing up?"

"Oh, so-so," Celia said. "Just wear one of your prettier dresses. We could be dancing."

"Dancing!" Madeline groaned.

"Yes. Charles is going, too, so I'll have a partner."

"Charles! A partner!"

"Madeline, I swear you sound like a parrot," Celia said, glancing quickly at her watch. "Gosh, I'm going to be late. Bye, love."

After her mother had driven away, Madeline took a deep breath and entered the house. If this was the way her life was going to be here with her mother, she didn't know if she could bear it. But then if Jake weren't renting that damn cabin all of this wouldn't be going on, she reasoned.

She went to the kitchen and warmed her coffee. It was a beautiful morning outside and she would have liked to drink her coffee on the back porch. But she was afraid Jake might see her out there and take it upon himself to join her. On the other hand she could go up to her bedroom and sit on the balcony. But it looked straight down at the cabin! How could she get the man out of her mind with her eyes on his front door?

Damn! Damn! Damn! Why had she ever come back to Louisiana? If she had stayed in Ozark she'd never have met Jake Hunter.

Trudging up the stairs she entered her bedroom, tossed pillows onto the four-poster and propped herself against them.

In a few minutes she would get up, dress and try to put her life in forward motion. The trouble was, she thought, sipping her coffee, that she couldn't seem to take a forward step without connecting it to the past.

Seven years ago she had looked at the future with joy. She had imagined her whole life stretching out before her, to do with whatever she decided. Love, marriage, children and maybe a career of her own thrown in on the side; those were her goals.

So far the only one she had managed to obtain was marriage and even that one accomplishment had ended in disaster—although, to be fair, it had not begun that way. Andrew had been everything most women look for in a man. Tall, blond, handsome and very smart. He had been raised in wealth and by the age of twenty-five he was already earning a huge salary of his own.

Madeline had met him through a mutual friend. He traveled often due to his job, and at first they saw each other only occasionally. But gradually their relationship developed and Madeline found herself in love for the first time in her life. When Andrew asked her to marry him she was floating on air.

She had never understood why her mother had not been very enthusiastic about the marriage. Celia had urged her to wait, had insisted that Andrew was the wrong kind of person for Madeline. But Madeline saw only her newfound love and the excitement of starting a life and family of her own.

Madeline smiled ruefully as she stared down into her coffee cup. Dear Mother, you saw it all the time. You saw the cold, selfish person beneath that smooth outer surface. Madeline only wished she had been as wise as her mother back then.

Instead she had gone into the marriage dreamy-eyed, knowing they would live happily ever after. Once the ink had dried on the marriage certificate Andrew had become a different person. He acted as if marriage gave him the right to dictate her life. At first she had thought his possessiveness was just an indication of the depth of his love, but after three years of subservience to him she began to think differently.

Yet when Madeline had become pregnant, Andrew seemed to change a bit for the better. All of his business peers had children; he wanted them too. He coddled Madeline and insisted she quit her job as a bookkeeper for a large department store. So Madeline gave up her job. Of course her family was more important, and with the idea of a new baby making Andrew so happy, she looked on their marriage with new eyes. Maybe the baby would bring them closer together. Maybe the baby would make Andrew become the passionate, attentive husband she had always wanted. So far all they had shared was a house and a bed.

Madeline lost the baby in the third month of pregnancy. She had been shattered. All her hopes for the future had been centered on that helpless little life growing within her. When she lost it, she lost a part of herself. The doctor said it was nothing to be alarmed about. Many first pregnancies ended in miscarriage. They could always try again.

Try again, Madeline thought dismally. She didn't want to think about the past, but being in Jake's arms last night, discovering how it felt to have him hold and kiss her made her realize just how closely the past was connected to the future. For how could she offer herself to a man when she was only half a woman?

Reluctantly Madeline allowed her thoughts to return to the past. She and Andrew had tried again, although it took over two years for her to become pregnant again. During that time Andrew had grown more and more frustrated. The whole thing had begun to prick his ego. As far as he was concerned, it was her fault she wasn't getting pregnant. He certainly wasn't sterile! And even though he didn't say it, she knew exactly what he felt. He blamed her for losing the first child. If she had done everything as well as he, she would have carried the baby full term.

Madeline had tried to block out all the guilt and the grief, but with Andrew constantly silently condemning her, she had become more and more dispirited. The sex they shared had turned into a functional, loveless act performed only for the sake of procreation. The idea of a baby, who might need her and return her love, had been the only thing that kept her hanging on to any kind of hope.

Madeline finally became pregnant again, but this time she lost the baby in the second month. Andrew had been out of town when the pains had begun. She had called a neighbor to drive her to the hospital. Later, she had hemorrhaged so badly that she had to be rushed into surgery.

After the second miscarriage and some more testing, Madeline had learned she would never be able to carry a child.

Upon arriving home, Andrew had become cold, aloof and accusing. He had looked at Madeline in a way that said, you're useless, I no longer want you. Celia had been there when she'd been released from the hospital, and Madeline had gone home with her mother to Natchitoches for two weeks to recover physically. Her marriage never recovered.

Madeline put down the coffee cup and rose from the bed. Walking out on the balcony, she leaned over the balustrade and breathed deeply. The morning was already warm, and humidity hung heavy in the air. Dew was still glistening on the grass, and birds squawked and chattered at the bird feeder. It was a beautiful day; that was the only thing she needed to think about now.

"Hey good lookin', when are you going to dress and come down from there?"

The sound of Jake's voice frightened her and her hand involuntarily flew to her throat. Madeline had completely forgotten that she wanted to avoid him. She was dressed in a scanty white satin gown. It was not the type of garment in which you let anyone, much less a man you hardly knew, see you. But Jake was staring up at her as though it was perfectly innocent of him to do so.

"Should I be in a hurry?" she asked. Last night she had thought it would be impossible even to face him, much less have a conversation with the man. But looking at him now changed all that. His wide smile was genuine and she could not help but react to it.

"Of course you should. I've just made a stack of toast and Mr. Miles won't help me eat it. Come share some with me," he invited.

"I've already eaten a biscuit," she hedged.

"It's cinnamon," he persisted. "With lots of butter and sugar."

She smiled in spite of herself. His grinning face was irresistible. It had been a long time since she had been around happiness or laughter. That fact, and Jake himself, pulled at her like a magnet.

"I'm not dressed," she said, feeling her cheeks burn.

"I won't argue with that," he drawled, "but if you insist I'll give you time to throw something over that beautiful white thing."

Blushing furiously now, she backed away from the railing. "All right," she finally agreed. "Give me a minute."

Chapter Four

The front door of the cabin opened before Madeline reached it. Jake was looking at her as if she were someone he had known for a long time and liked very much. It made her feel good and self-conscious at the same time.

"Shucks, you did cover it up after all," he said with exaggerated disappointment. "I thought you might take pity on me and wear the gown anyway."

Madeline saw that he was looking at the white plissé robe she had thrown over the indecent nightgown. It was high-necked and ankle-length, but from Jake's expression you would have thought he could see right through it.

"You don't look as if you need to be pitied," she said.

He laughed as she entered the cabin. Its interior was dark and cool, thanks to the air-conditioning unit humming in the window. Madeline quickly glanced around her, noticing the changes Jake had made. The little guest house consisted primarily of two rooms, the front serving as living and kitchen area while the back was a bedroom with a bath just off it. Jake had pushed the dinette table away from the window and replaced it with a heavy oak desk that was now piled with a jumbled mess of papers, a computer and an old manual typewriter. There was other evidence of his profession, including an enormous number of books and papers stacked on a row of metal shelves. The room, on the whole, was rather messy. Untidiness usually bothered Madeline; funny that it didn't annoy her now. To be honest, she rather liked the atmosphere Jake had given the old cabin.

It was obvious a person lived and worked in the little house. There were several papers that had been wadded, then tossed toward the wastebasket at the side of his desk. Some of them had hit their mark, others hadn't and had been ignored. She imagined Jake, unsatisfied with what he had written, angrily crumbling the papers in frustration. He may not be much of a housekeeper, but she somehow preferred this cluttered little cabin to the spotless house she had shared with Andrew.

"Coffee?" he asked as Madeline seated herself at the little wooden table.

He was standing behind the short bar that separated the living area from the kitchen area. Madeline looked at him and smiled. "Have you learned to make good Louisiana coffee yet?"

He grinned as he poured two mugs full. "I'm trying, but blending different types of coffee just isn't my thing. As long as it has caffeine in it, I like it."

He carried the coffee and a plate of toast to the table. It gave off a delicious aroma, and she found she was much hungrier now than she had been earlier.

"This looks good," she told him, taking a couple of pieces of the toast. "Do you cook often?"

"Whenever it's necessary. I have to admit Celia has spoiled me. She throws me all her leftovers."

Yes, she would, Madeline thought. Her mother seemed to think very highly of Jake. She took a bite of the toast and enjoyed the taste of the sugar and melted butter.

"Actually, I had all sorts of reasons for inviting you over this morning," Jake said.

Madeline looked at him suspiciously. She couldn't imagine what he had on his mind. After last night she was afraid even to think about it. What would she do if he thought she was a love-starved divorcée ready to jump into any man's bed?

"Oh?" she said with forced lightness.

"Yes," he answered, lifting the coffee mug to his lips.

Madeline watched him with womanly pleasure. He was a piece of masculine perfection that would be hard for any female to ignore. Apparently he had recently gotten out of the shower. His hair was still damp, giving it a sleek appearance and making it seem almost black. The shirt he wore tucked into his jeans was made of yellow oxford cloth and the color contrasted vividly with his deeply tanned skin. He wore the sleeves rolled up on his forearms and his gold watch glinted in the light as he placed the mug back on the table.

"I wanted to apologize for making you cry last night."

She breathed deeply while thinking back to last evening after he had brought her home. He had merely walked her to the door and given her a soft, almost brotherly, goodnight kiss. She had been ever so grateful to him.

"You didn't make me cry," she told him, lowering her eyes from his face. "I made myself do that."

"Still," he said gently. "I didn't like seeing you so distraught. That wasn't my intention at all."

She was too afraid to ask what his intentions had been. Instead she lifted her gaze back to his face. "What were the other reasons you asked me over?" she questioned quickly, wanting to forget their shared kisses.

He grinned slyly now and Madeline shifted uneasily in her seat.

"To ask if you knew shorthand."

She stared at him in complete surprise. Whatever she had expected from him, it had been nothing like this! "Yes, but it's been a while since I used it. I'd be rather slow at it."

"Speed isn't essential," he said eagerly. He reached for another piece of toast. "I'll take your help at any speed."

"My help?"

He nodded. "There is going to be so much historical fact in this book that I'm finding it a problem organizing all the places, dates and names. And I'd be spending the next three months in the library if I wrote it in longhand."

She leaned back in her chair, beginning to comprehend his problem. "And of course the more valuable historical documents can't be checked out for personal use."

"Exactly. If you agree, we could go together and I'd show you things I need and you could take them down in shorthand."

She reached for her coffee, a smile on her face. "And then, of course, I'd have to decipher and type the shorthand out for you."

He chuckled. "Like I said, you attracted me right from the start."

Madeline ignored his words and said, "I am planning on starting my dress shop soon. How much help do you need? I mean for how long?"

"Weeks! Months! As much time as you can spare," he said, looking at her intently. She was just as beautiful as she had been yesterday, even wearing that damn virginal robe and with her face devoid of makeup. She had the most exquisite green eyes he had ever seen, but try as he might he could not read the thoughts behind them. It left him feeling both challenged and frustrated. "Of course I'll pay you whatever you require."

Surprised, she let out a breath. On the one hand, the idea of having something interesting to do with her free time was very appealing, but on the other, how could she trust her emotions if she became the constant companion of Jake Hunter? "Well," she said, "I suppose I could help you until the sale of my house goes through or I obtain a loan."

He was ashamed to find he was glad she was not wealthy. Then he told his conscience that once he had things going the way he wanted them to go he would make sure she had her dress shop, even if he had to give her the money outright. Hell, he'd give her the money now if he thought she would take it, but he already knew enough about this woman to realize she would never accept. Besides, he was selfish, he admitted to himself. He wanted some time with her, one way or another.

"Good," he said, and smiled suddenly. "We'll start today. How about now, after we eat?"

"Now!" she blurted. "Jake, give me time to digest all this."

"But Maddie, I'm behind schedule. Lord, am I ever behind schedule!"

Madeline didn't know why she sympathized with his problem. He had probably never been poor a day in his life while she had no income as of now. In fact, all she had in the world was what she had gotten in the divorce settlement. She was the one behind schedule!

"I promised Mother I'd call about the place on Front Street. And then I'm going to see a friend," she told him.

Her final words brought a frown to his face. "A friend? He or she?"

She shook her head in disbelief. "Are you sure you're not a lawyer instead of a writer?" She had never seen anyone who could directly or indirectly lead and maneuver like this man. "The friend is a she," Madeline went on. "A former employer who owns a dress shop over in the business district."

"Good," he said, his gray eyes gleaming as he watched her. "I'll drive you over. There are several things I need to pick up."

Madeline wasn't sure about any of this. He was going too fast for her. She was the kind of person who took things step by step. How could she do that when he was always one step ahead of her?

Without commenting she finished her toast and the last swallow of her coffee. At the same time Jake rose from the table saying, "What was the name of that law firm? Gable, Gunther or something like that?"

She watched him as he walked to the telephone. What was he doing now? "You mean the one on Front Street?"

"Yes. The one in the building you want."

"I don't remember exactly. Why?"

He picked up the telephone directory and began to leaf through it. "Here it is," he said, then looked at her. "Now tell me, what do you plan to spend in terms of rent?"

Madeline rose swiftly from her chair. "I don't know. I haven't really thought about it. What are you doing?" she asked, hurrying over to him. She already knew him well enough to expect the unexpected.

"I'm going to call them for you." He reached for the telephone, but Madeline reacted quickly and pushed his hand away from the receiver.

"No! They don't know you! I'm the one who's going to be in the business, not you!" she cried. The man was unbelievable!

"Now, Maddie darling, calm down," he said in a gravelly drawl. "The fact that they don't know me is all to your advantage. I'm just going to act like your lawyer. It's much better to go through legal connections. Gives a person the right image. You'll have a better chance of getting it this way."

His words, which were meant to calm her, only served to alarm her even further. "Jake, you're insane! You are not going to do this! I won't let you!"

He laughed, took her by the arms and led her to the low-slung couch at the opposite side of the room. "Sit and watch a pro in action." He pushed her down on the cushions, then back down again when Madeline bounced to her feet.

"Jake, if you mess things up for me, I'll—I'll—" She couldn't think of a vile enough threat.

He chuckled even more, as though it amused him to see her so flustered and angry. "If I lose the place for you, then I'll buy you a steamboat and you can sell dresses up and down the river from here to New Orleans," he promised.

She groaned instead of uttering the few choice words clinging to her tongue. "You're crazy! No wonder you use a pseudonym!"

He was dialing the number, laughing all the while at her words, and she realized that nothing seemed to anger the man.

When he began to speak to the party at the other end of the line, Madeline sat on the edge of the couch nervously twisting her fingers. She couldn't believe the man's audacity. He was charm itself as he informed the secretary he was Ms. Madeline Beaumont's advisor, then went on to inquire about a lease to the second floor.

Madeline was flabbergasted as Jake proceeded to stress what an asset the dress shop would be to Front Street and that he could assure them that Ms. Beaumont was a competent businesswoman.

In spite of everything she couldn't help being exuberant when she heard him say, "That sounds agreeable. Just send the information to my address and Ms. Beaumont and I will be happy to review it. Yes, it's been a pleasure doing business with you. Good day.''

"How was I?" he asked with so much conceit that Madeline giggled.

"I was right about the first impression I had of you. Car thief or con artist—you fit the last one beautifully."

He approached her, lifted her hand and ceremoniously kissed the back of it. "Ms. Madeline Beaumont, stick with me and you will soon become the lessee of the second floor of a building on Front Street. The law firm plans on vacating in twelve weeks. By then you'll have a contract in your hands. By the way, you may have your choice of a one-year or three-year contract. Payment due when they move out and you move in.''

"Twelve weeks!" She jumped to her feet and found herself standing mere inches from him. "Jake! What will I do if the house doesn't sell or if I can't get a loan? What have you done to me, you idiot? Have you committed me?''

Last night he had discovered the passion hidden behind her cool exterior. It pleased him to see it again as he watched the fire dance in her green eyes. A self-satisfied smile on his face, he said, "Yes. Don't you think I deserve a kiss?''

"A kiss!" She gasped in total disbelief. "I should kill you!''

He frowned perplexedly. "But I thought you wanted the place? You seemed to have your heart set on it.''

"I did! I do! But I'm not like you, Jake. I'm not made of money!''

He reached out and touched her hair. It was beautiful hair. Soft, silky and it smelled of gardenias. As it brushed against her shoulders it seemed, to him, like a teasing red flame.

"Maddie," he said placatingly. "Don't get so worked up. Everything will be fine, trust me. I'll get you the lease, and if need be I can get you the rest.''

His last words frightened her. Somehow they sounded far too personal. It was then that she finally realized how close she was standing to him, so close that she could see the faint lines at the corners of his eyes and mouth, the soft dark hair curling around the edge of his shirt where it veed against his dark throat. He smelled of exotic spices, the same way he had smelled the night before, and suddenly she remembered how wonderful it had been to have his arms around her, his lips upon hers. The memory caused a chill to run through her. Kiss him? She wanted to do that now more than she had ever wanted anything in her life.

"I hope you're right, Jake. Because if you aren't, I'll never forgive you. Furthermore, since you're my new lawyer or advisor or something, I'll give you the embarrassing job of telling them I'm broke."

He chuckled and Madeline shivered when his thumb and forefinger caressed and finally tugged on her earlobe. "It's going to be wonderful living with a redhead."

Living! He did it again! Was there no stopping the man? "I think the word is working, not living," she corrected primly.

"Give me time, Maddie, just a little time," he murmured, a crooked grin on his lips.

Madeline didn't give him time for anything. She rushed out the door, telling him she'd be ready to go to Maria's in an hour.

Even though Jake's Cadillac was old, it rode like a dream, and with the top down, the breeze was a cool delight.

Madeline looked at the traffic and shops eagerly. It was hard to believe this was only her second day home. So much had happened in such a short time.

After she had left Jake to dress, she had gone over the whole scene with him in her mind. It had struck her as deliriously funny, and she had giggled while she applied her makeup.

She had been so hostile and he had been so smug and amused. She had to admit he was infuriating, but she also had to admit he made her feel alive. It had been ages since she had gotten excited about anything. She wondered if Jake realized that.

Jake momentarily took his eyes off the traffic to glance at Madeline. She was dressed in an emerald-green shift trimmed with white piping, and the wind was whipping her hair around her face. He wondered at her soft, secretive smile.

"Can you let me in on it?"

She turned at the sound of his voice. "I beg your pardon?"

"The smile on your face," he explained. "You seemed to be amused about something."

"I was," she admitted. "You."

"Me?"

"And the fact that you took it upon yourself to become my ... well, my lawyer, I guess. So far you've acted as a mechanic, writer and now lawyer. Should I be prepared for anything else?"

"You left out car thief and con man," he said.

Still smiling, she looked back out the window. "I can't wait to see what's next."

"I thought you were angry with me," he said, goading her.

She shrugged, conceding to herself that it was hard to stay angry with him. He had only been trying to help her. Andrew had never involved himself in any of her interests. It felt good that this man seemed to care about her.

"I've decided that since the great Harlon Howard is on my side, I probably have nothing to worry about."

"That's what I like to hear, dear Maddie. Implicit faith."
He smiled and winked at her. "And you're going to learn
that from the first moment you stepped into this Cadillac,
you picked the right man to trust."

"That will take some doing," she said, while tugging
down the hem of her skirt. It would have been far safer to
wear slacks, she thought, as Jake seemed to find the shape
of her legs more interesting than the traffic in front of him.
She didn't know whether to be flattered or offended.

He let her out at Maria's store and went on about his
business. As she watched him pull away from the curb,
Madeline suddenly felt very confused. She had met him only
yesterday but already he was firmly planted in her life and
her thoughts. It was dangerous. It was not a thing she
should want. But she could not stop wanting Jake, and she
knew she couldn't possibly stop him.

"Madeline! How wonderful to see you again!"

A small, dark-haired woman hurried toward her. Smiling, she hugged Madeline fiercely, then inspected her with
sharp black eyes.

"Goodness, Madeline, you've grown even more beautiful over the years! Are you here to stay or just visiting?"

Madeline shook her head and let her gaze wander around
the clothing boutique. It was filled with the newest fashions, expensive bottles of perfume and an array of elegant
jewelry. Apparently Maria had not lost her knack for success.

"I'm here to stay. I suppose Mother hasn't told you I'm
divorced now." Madeline shrugged. "She wanted me to
come back home to Natchitoches and I agreed with her. I've
always loved it here."

"Of course your mother would want you here with her,"
Maria exclaimed, then lightly touched Madeline's arm. "Do

you have time for coffee? Let's go back to my office. Rose-
anna will take care of the customers."

Madeline noticed a pretty blond woman who was busy
showing swim wear to a couple of teenage girls. It had been
a long time since Madeline had worked in the same capac-
ity for Maria. Even so, she could still remember how satisfying the work had been to her. It had been fun meeting new
people every day and making new friends, and she had loved
the excitement of the ever-changing fashions.

"You know, I've always kept up with you through your
mother. I'm sorry to hear about your divorce. I remember
how infatuated you were with Andrew."

The two of them walked through an open door and into
a small room furnished with a desk and filing cabinets, a
couch and two armchairs. It was cluttered, just as it had
been when Madeline had last seen it seven years ago.

Madeline did her best to keep the tight grimace from her
face as Maria reminded her of her foolishness about Andrew. "Don't be sorry," she said as Maria handed her a
small cup of black coffee. "It—well, Andrew and I will be
much happier apart."

Both women sat on the maroon couch. Madeline noticed
the years had been kind to Maria. She had to be at least fifty
now, yet there was scarcely a wrinkle on her face.

"As long as you're happy." Maria smiled understand-
ingly. "That's all that matters."

"To tell you the truth, I've got it in my head to try my
hand at my own clothing shop. What do you think? Just
women's fashions, of course."

Maria laughed heartily and sipped her coffee. "I'd say
I'm worried. You'd give me stiff competition."

Madeline blushed. "Maria, you don't need to flatter me.
I know how long it takes to build up a name and a steady
clientele."

"That's true. But I also know you were the only assistant I ever had who knew instinctively what a customer would like."

Madeline smiled gratefully at the older woman. It had been a long time since anyone other than Celia had told her she had talent of any kind. "You say it like that's all I need."

Maria laughed "It is," she insisted. "That and the money to start on."

Madeline sighed. "Yes, well, I'm working on that part of it. And as of today it seems I'm getting a store on Front Street." Thanks to Jake, she added silently. Too bad Andrew never could get results as fast as Jake Hunter, but then she knew it was ridiculous to compare the two men. They were as different as ice and fire.

Maria's brows arched with speculation. "How lucky! Just think of the tourist trade you might pick up."

"That's what I'm hoping," Madeline agreed.

The two women discussed the business a bit further. Maria gave her sound advice on some problems Madeline might find herself dealing with, then they wandered back out to the boutique.

She and Maria were inspecting the latest shipment of skirts and dresses when the bell over the shop door tinkled.

Madeline glanced up to see Jake strolling toward them. The sight of him suddenly reminded her how long she had been talking. He must have been waiting for ages!

"Maddie darling, I hate to disturb you, but my Goo Goo bars are melting," he whispered next to her ear, a wry grin on his face.

Madeline took one look at the sparkle in his gray eyes, then hurriedly glanced at Maria, who was watching intently only a few feet away. After this morning she didn't know what to expect of him. Anything could roll out of the man's mouth!

"I'm sorry," she apologized in a low voice, then said more loudly, "Maria, this is my—er, friend, Jake Hunter."

Maria studied Jake with obvious pleasure. "How do you do?" she inquired politely.

Jake nodded and took the woman's offered hand. "Nice to meet you," he drawled. "I hope you ladies had a nice visit?"

"Very nice," she assured him. "I've missed Madeline since she moved to Ozark. It's wonderful to hear she's back in Natchitoches to stay."

"My sentiments exactly," Jake said, his arm moving to rest lightly on the back of Madeline's waist.

Maria's glance went from Jake's affectionate gesture to Madeline's pink cheeks. "Are you just visiting Natchitoches this summer?" she asked.

Jake opened his mouth to reply, but Madeline quickly stated, "Jake has leased the cabin from Mother. He's researching the history of our area."

Jake smiled dryly at Madeline's flushed face. "I'm a writer," he explained to Maria.

"How wonderful," Maria exclaimed, then added, "I hope you have a nice stay here in our city."

"I'm sure I will. Natchitoches is becoming more interesting every day," Jake said, and then gave Madeline a gentle nudge toward the door. "Perhaps we'll meet again."

"Yes," Maria insisted. "And Madeline, I'll be looking forward to seeing you again very soon. I'll give you all your dos and don'ts."

Madeline smiled and waved at her former employer as they passed through the door. "Thank you. Goodbye, Maria."

The sun was blazing down on the Cadillac. Once in the car Jake grabbed up a package and gently poked a finger at the contents. When he groaned and crammed the package out of sight beneath the seat Madeline didn't have to be told what was inside it.

"I take it that was your Goo Goo bars," Madeline said regretfully while settling herself upon the hot upholstery.

"What's left of them," he answered and quickly started the engine.

"I'm sorry," she told him as he backed out of the parking area. "You should have come in for me sooner."

Jake laughed and looked at her as though he couldn't believe she expected him to be angry. "Maddie, don't sound so contrite. I'm not angry with you. Why in the world should I be?"

"But you must have been waiting for an hour! I—we got to discussing the clothing business and time got away from me."

He shrugged, reached over and patted her hand. "I'm not an impatient man. Besides, I'll get all that time back when I put you to work."

Madeline smiled as the car began to pick up speed. "I'll buy you some more candy bars," she offered. It was a relief to find him so calm. Always when she had inadvertently kept Andrew waiting he had responded with cold fury. But she was swiftly learning that Jake was not like Andrew Spencer in any way; he was not like any other man at all.

Jake's chuckle rippled away on the wind. "I'll stick these in the fridge. By the time we get back from the library they'll be hard enough to eat. We'll have a chocolate orgy."

"The library!" She glanced over to see the wind tugging his dark hair away from his forehead. His rugged face held a dangerous charm for Madeline. She found she wanted to look at it constantly.

"Well, yes," he drawled as if the day ahead of them was theirs for the taking. "Won't you be ready?"

She stared at him as she tried to wriggle into a more comfortable position. How could the man appear so laid-back when actually he was always on the run? "Why, I don't know why not," she told him dryly, thinking of her suitcases still piled in the middle of her bedroom floor. "I mean, after all, I've been here less than twenty-four hours. That's oodles of time to get settled in!"

"That's what I thought," he agreed with a beguiling smile. "Any more time than that would just be a waste. So we'll grab a quick lunch at the cabin, then drive over to the library. You're going to be fascinated," he said, then looked at her and winked. "I promise."

She smiled ironically. Yes, more than likely she would be fascinated—with him, not the historical facts.

Madeline knew that if she had any sense at all she would get out of this Cadillac as quickly as she could, pack her suitcases and head right out of town. But where would she go? Back to Ozark? Or maybe to some strange city where no one would know her?

She glanced at Jake's handsome, relaxed face. The traitorous surge of her heart assured her she was headed straight for trouble.

Chapter Five

"Madeline?"

"In here, Mother. I'm in the tub."

Celia poked her head around the bathroom door to see her daughter up to her neck in bubbles. Her red hair was tied high up on the back of her head with a blue ribbon. The few strands that had managed to escape hung dangerously close to Madeline's wet shoulders.

"I just wanted to let you know I was home," her mother told her, then added with some surprise, "I thought you would be dressed by now."

Madeline gave her a look of dismay. "I would have been, but Jake just decided to come home a few minutes ago."

Celia pushed the door open further and entered the steamy bathroom. "You've been out with Jake?" she asked curiously.

Madeline squeezed the rose-colored washcloth so that the hot sudsy water could slide down her tired back. "Mother, I think I've become a complete idiot," she muttered.

"Somehow, some way, I've managed to find myself scratching down notes in shorthand and typing not only them, but rough drafts of Jake's manuscript. That's not even counting the two trips we made to the college library."

Celia smiled as she began to undo the knotted blue silk at her throat. "So Jake's put you to work?"

Madeline nodded. "I'm still not quite sure how he talked me into it."

Her mother chuckled softly. "It comes easy for Jake."

Madeline didn't reply and Celia glanced at her daughter's face. "Why, don't you think you'll enjoy it? I would think working with a marvelous talent like Jake would be exciting."

Madeline shrugged and sank lower into the hot water. "It is very interesting," she conceded. "And I did enjoy it. But I—"

She broke off in confusion and Celia studied her daughter thoughtfully. "What, Maddie? You look so—troubled."

Madeline looked up at her mother. "I am, Mother. This is only my second day home. I should be giving all my attention to planning the dress shop, making out a budget I can live with and deciding just how soon I can go to Dallas on a buying trip. But am I? No! Instead, my time and my thoughts are consumed with Jake Hunter. And that's not all. He already has tomorrow and the next day planned out and the day after, and—"

Celia smiled faintly. "Madeline, give yourself time. This past year has been tough on you. You need time away from everything. Helping Jake will give you a different look at life. There's no need to rush into the responsibilities of a new business the first week you're home. You'll have plenty of time for it later. So relax and enjoy yourself. You weren't always a worried, serious woman who never smiled or laughed."

Madeline sighed and pulled the plug from the drain. "I guess I've changed, Mom. I guess Andrew squashed the happy, carefree girl I once was."

Celia pulled a bath sheet from a glass rack and handed it to Madeline. She quickly wrapped it around her.

"Then you must find her again, darling," Celia said gently. "For your own sake, you've got to search and find her again."

A tiny smile flickered across Madeline's face. "Jake is fun to be around," she admitted. "He's very interesting. And it's so nice to see someone with so much intelligence who still has a sense of humor about himself."

Celia's worried look swiftly vanished, and she started toward the door. "I know what you mean. Furthermore, I think Jake's attitude is exactly what you need to get you out of these doldrums."

"I hope so," Madeline said, but doubt filled her thoughts as her mother shut the door behind her. What Celia didn't know was that besides being fun, Jake was also dangerous. Madeline was in no position to get involved with a man. She was afraid if she stayed around Jake much longer she would be in danger of losing her heart to him.

Charles Ramone arrived at the Beaumont house long before Madeline or Celia was dressed and ready to go. Luckily, Jake was downstairs in the drawing room to greet him, offer him a drink, and keep him company.

Charles lived only a short distance down the street. He had moved there around the time Madeline had married Andrew seven years before. He was a widower, warm and friendly and still quite handsome even though he was in his late sixties. His Mexican ancestry had given him dark skin and black hair that was just now beginning to show threads of silver.

Madeline had guessed a long time ago that Charles was extremely fond of her mother. She even suspected he would marry her if Celia could be persuaded to try it. But Madeline knew her mother enjoyed her independence. Charles would have a hard row to hoe if he ever attempted to change Celia's mind.

Jake had made dinner reservations at Lasyone's, a French restaurant located just a few blocks away in the historical district. A nationally known restaurant, Lasyone's was a haunt of the rich and famous. She supposed Jake Hunter could now be added to the long list of celebrities who had visited the restaurant.

He drove all four of them over in his Cadillac, and gallantly remembered to put the top up so that the wind wouldn't blow Madeline's and Celia's hair.

Madeline had piled her red mane on top of her head, and when she had appeared downstairs in a white sleeveless sweater dress Jake had told her she looked very regal. Now, as he sat beside her in Lasyone's, she could have told him he looked very dashing, even though he was merely dressed in a white shirt, dark slacks and a tie. For a man who seemed to wear nothing but jeans and casual shirts, Madeline supposed this must be a big concession. She tried to picture him in a tuxedo at some elegant affair but found the going very difficult. He was too much of a diamond in the rough.

"Is everyone going to have the specialty of the house, or does someone want something different?" Jake asked as they sipped wine and the waitress arrived to take their orders.

"The specialty sounds fine to me," Charles announced and the others agreed.

The waitress left and Madeline let her eyes roam around the room. The restaurant was actually just a big two-story, Bourbon Street-type house, nothing glitzy or glamorous. It was known for its good food, not the decor. The four of them had been placed in one of the smaller rooms, and Madeline liked it because it was cozy and private.

"I want to make a toast to my new secretary," Jake said. "With her help I'm going to get this book finished in record time."

Charles and Celia seconded him loudly while Madeline merely groaned.

"It took me an hour to decipher one page of my rusty shorthand," she told them.

"But you didn't miss any of the information I needed," Jake insisted proudly. "And that's the important thing." He raised his glass again and smiled at Madeline. "And I think we should also drink to Maddie's good news. Have you told them?"

Madeline shook her head, and Jake said rather smugly, "It looks like Maddie is going to get the lease on the building. Her dress shop will soon be on Front Street."

"Madeline! That's wonderful!" Celia exclaimed.

"It certainly is," Charles added. "That was quite a bit of luck. How did you manage it?"

Madeline grinned wryly at Jake. "Ask my legal consultant here. He can tell you all about it."

Jake chuckled but did not go into detail. "Maddie, dear, you've got to learn that you can't go around divulging your business tactics. You might want to use them again." He looked at Celia and Charles. "Really all I did was make a phone call. It even looks like they'll give her the option of a one-year or three-year lease."

"Oh, I'd take the three. It will take more than a year to get a business going," Celia suggested.

Madeline didn't respond to her mother's remarks. Something like that couldn't be decided until she was certain about her finances.

"What are you going to name it, Madeline?" Charles asked.

The question stumped her. "I hadn't really thought about it. Not anything outlandish. Just something that will be easy to remember." She looked at Jake. "You're a man who deals with titles. Give me one."

"Easy," he said without hesitation. "I'd simply call it Madeline's. It has a glamorous ring to it. Goes right along with the owner," he murmured devilishly.

Madeline blushed, especially as she saw the smiles exchanged by her mother and Charles.

"I don't know. I'll think about it," she hedged. Actually, she wasn't used to being the center of attention, and she certainly wasn't used to having men like Jake Hunter give her compliments.

Glamorous! Was the woman sitting here in this restaurant the same despondent woman that Andrew had called frigid and useless? Madeline wondered. How could Jake see her so differently? Perhaps it was simply because he didn't know about her, she thought. He didn't know that she could never give him or any man a child, could never be the kind of woman a man would want as a wife.

Madeline clenched her wineglass as sadness filled her. She looked away from Jake and stared down at the tabletop. Why did she have to think of this now? Why did she have to be this way at all? Why couldn't she have been a whole, normal woman who could offer herself to a man without guilt or regret?

Her hand shook slightly as she brought the glass to her lips. Her heart kept crying, *Don't let me love him, because I can never be Jake's woman*.

"Maddie, did you hear that? Your mother said one of the tellers came up five thousand short today."

Jake's rough drawl pulled her out of her miserable thoughts, and she glanced up, realizing her mind had carried her far away. She forced herself to smile. She was over being sorry for herself. She was going to be happy. She would make herself be happy.

"Did they find it?" she asked.

"After about two hours of searching," Celia answered. "The amount of a check had been copied down wrong. But by then, the poor girl was in tears."

At that moment their food arrived and everyone began to enjoy the meat pies the restaurant was famous for. Served with them was a dish Louisians called dirty rice, which was unbleached rice, boiled and smothered with rich brown gravy.

Madeline was stuffed by the time they left the restaurant. She couldn't believe the other three could think about dancing after having eaten such huge meals.

"It'll work off all those calories," her mother insisted and Madeline gave up trying to argue with them.

Jake drove them to a club that featured a live band and slow, easy music. They had barely found a table when Charles and Celia left them for the dance floor. Madeline fidgeted with her glass of soda water and Jake lit a cigarette, leaned back in his chair and looked at her through the smoky haze.

"You don't have to be so worried about stepping on my toes, you know," he said.

Madeline glanced at him and took a deep breath. "What makes you think I'm worried?" she asked, trying to keep her voice light.

"It was obvious you didn't want to come here."

She shrugged and nervously played with the pearls at her throat. "It's been a long day."

He took a drag of his cigarette. "Yes. And I've enjoyed it."

Madeline watched the smoke escape his lips and nostrils, wondering what it was about this man that made her so sexually aware of him, and herself.

She studied the smooth, tanned skin of his face and decided that if he should ever choose not to shave, he would have a heavy beard. She could easily imagine the short stubbly shadow that would cover his jaw early in the morning. She even knew how it would feel against her own cheek, rough and exciting.

"I—I have, too," she replied, trying her best to fight the images running through her mind. Did she inspire the same kind of ideas in him? No, she couldn't, she silently assured herself. There was nothing especially exciting about Madeline Beaumont.

She glanced quickly over the dimly lighted dance floor. Celia and Charles were still dancing, obviously enjoying the music and each other. However, Madeline wished they would come back to the table. This atmosphere was too romantic, too intimate for her to be left alone with Jake.

The next thing she knew, Jake was stubbing out his cigarette and reaching for her hand.

"How long has it been since you danced, Maddie?"

Madeline turned her face to his and looked into his gray eyes. The question she saw in them was more like, How long has it been since you've made love? She shivered ever so slightly as her fingers curled around his.

"A very long time, Jake. I'd probably smash your toes."

He grinned rather seductively and pulled her to her feet. "I'll take my chances. My insurance premium is paid up."

Madeline smiled with dry amusement as he led her out onto the dance floor. Too bad there wasn't some kind of emotional insurance she could take out as a protection against this man.

"You know, when Celia first told me you were coming back here, I really wasn't looking forward to it," he said, taking her gently into the curve of his arm.

Madeline's hand came up to rest upon his shoulder. It felt wonderful to be in his arms again, so wonderful that she didn't even want to speak.

"Why?" she asked simply.

His expression was sheepish. "I thought because you were Celia's daughter she probably wasn't telling me the whole story. I figured, she's young and divorced, so more than likely irresponsible and wild."

Madeline wanted to laugh, for those adjectives were so off base it was actually comical. "So, even if that had been true, it still shouldn't have affected you."

"Maddie dear, sometimes it's hard for me to believe you've been married and lived out in the world. All women don't look at me like you do. Most of them see money and fame where I'm concerned."

Her green eyes glinted as she smiled back at him. "And how do you think I look at you?"

His lips pursed thoughtfully. "I think you just see a rascal that you wish you didn't have to deal with."

She actually giggled, making Jake grin broadly. "That feeling has hit me several times since I met you," she admitted.

His fingers moved slowly, seductively against her back. Madeline realized she shouldn't have worn something so revealing. At least then she wouldn't know how pleasant his fingers felt against her skin.

"I've had quite a few feelings hit me, too, since I met you," he told her. Some of them had been very alien to him, he realized as he looked down at the beautiful woman in his arms. He had never known the fierce protectiveness he felt for Madeline. He had never known this constant urge to make her smile, to know that she was happy and that he alone was the reason for her happiness. He realized that for the first time in his life he was actually falling in love.

The fact scared him. Not because he was afraid of being tied down, or afraid to commit himself. But because he knew that this woman had been hurt terribly. It was obvious she was disillusioned with marriage, maybe even with men altogether. He was going to have to tread lightly, he decided. He was going to have to find out just what had hurt her and make it all right again.

Yet she felt so soft and desirable in his arms. How was he going to be able to curb his urge to crush her in his arms and kiss her senseless? He was already in trouble. He knew it, but there was nothing he could do about it now.

Madeline was afraid to ask him what kind of feelings she had inspired in him. Instead she said, "Jake, have you ever been married?"

He glanced down at her, surprise on his face. "No, I came close once, but it didn't happen."

She looked over his shoulder, part of her mind aware of the soft lighting of the room and the gentle rhythm of the music; the other part was imagining Jake with another woman. She hated the image and was shocked to realize the only woman she wanted to picture in Jake's arms was herself.

"Why?"

He shrugged and pulled her even closer to him. Madeline felt her breasts yield softly against his hard chest.

"It just didn't work out. We had completely different sets of values," he answered.

She shook her head. "No. I mean, why do you think you've never married?"

They traveled several steps around the dance floor before he finally answered. "I guess it's because I'm basically an old-fashioned person. My views on marriage don't agree with most people's. I decided a long time ago that if I ever married, I wanted to have a marriage like my mother and father's. They were loving, sharing, totally committed to each other. That's not an easy thing to find these days.''

''Yes, I know. I tried and failed.''

He'd been resting his cheek against her hair, but now he pulled back in order to study her face.

''Do you always measure everything in terms of success or failure?''

His question threw her, because it made her aware that she did do just that. ''It's hard not to,'' she told him. ''When everything you've put your heart into has failed abysmally.''

He sighed. ''Madeline, just because a person experiences failure doesn't mean everything stops. It doesn't mean his life is over.''

''Oh sure,'' she said dryly. ''Words right out of the great Harlon Howard's mouth. But how would you know? When have you ever failed at anything?''

He grimaced with exasperation. ''Sometimes I don't know whether to shake you or kiss you.''

Her eyes were drawn to his, and she couldn't understand why she should be thinking about his beautiful dark lashes at a time like this. The man was scolding her, yet her mind was wandering. Was she already that hopelessly lost? The idea made her angry with herself.

''That's funny, because I have the same feelings toward you,'' she retorted, surprising them both.

The music ended, but instead of leading her back to the table, Jake held her tightly and waited until the next song started.

''My darling, you are so confused about me,'' he said once they had started to dance again.

Amen, Madeline silently agreed but said nothing.

''The great Harlon Howard, as you call me, hasn't always been a success. Before I became a bestselling author, I had a whole slew of rejections and failures.''

She stared at him in total disbelief.

"It's true," he insisted. "I started out trying to write short stories, hoping to sell to some major magazines. It wasn't as easy as I thought. After about two dozen rejection slips, I said this just isn't going to cut it. So, I thought about it long and hard and decided my characters were the problem. They were the kind that needed room to grow and deepen and I couldn't do that in only a few short pages."

"What did you do?" Madeline asked, trying to imagine Jake, the picture of success, going through the frustration of a long list of failures.

"I ate a lot of bologna and gave all my friends a good laugh. I started on a novel, and everyone said, my Lord, Jake's gone mad! He can't even sell a short story and now he thinks he's going to be the great American novelist!"

Madeline chuckled. "Well, you must have either been very crazy or very brave," she said.

He laughed along with her. "Probably a bit of both, if the truth were known. But at least I proved to everyone, including myself, that I wasn't a failure. I was just in the wrong pew."

She made a face at him. "Am I supposed to be getting a moral lesson from this?"

He reached up to give her chin a gentle shake. "The moral is, Maddie, that you shouldn't think you've failed as a person just because your marriage didn't work out. You were probably just like me, in the wrong place at the wrong time, with the wrong person."

She felt tears sting her eyes as she looked into his strong, reassuring face. He was being so kind. And it touched her deeply, more deeply than he would ever know. Andrew, the man who had once professed to love her, had never taken the effort to bolster her ego. But here was Jake, a man she was just beginning to know, doing his best to convince her she was a good, worthwhile person. She couldn't believe he could actually care that much.

"Oh, Jake," she murmured, and pressed her face against his neck. She wanted to say, I love you, hold me close, never let me go. The words were in her throat, burning, clawing, begging to be released, but Madeline swallowed them and instead whispered brokenly, "I—I'm so glad I came home."

The words must have been enough for him because the hand upon her back pressed her tightly against him. Madeline's fingers curled responsively around the back of his neck.

Tonight she would hold on and enjoy him. Tomorrow she would worry about the condition of her heart.

Chapter Six

The next morning Madeline was lifting the coffeepot to pour herself a cup when the telephone rang.

Celia put down the egg turner she was holding and picked up the receiver. "Hello?"

Madeline glanced at her mother while trying to figure who would be calling at such an early hour. The next words Celia spoke gave her the answer.

"Oh, hello Jake. Yes, she is up. Would you like to speak with her?"

While Celia listened to his reply, Madeline set her still-empty cup down on the cabinet. By now she didn't care about the coffee. She was remembering how wonderful it had been to be with Jake last night. As they had danced she'd realized she'd begun to care for him very deeply, and this morning she knew her feelings were still just as strong. She loved Jake. For better or worse, she loved him.

"Of course I'll tell her," Celia went on. "See you later, Jake."

Her mother hung up the telephone and looked at Madeline. "Jake says if you're going to work for him to get your clothes on and get over there. He's cooking ham and grits."

"Ham and grits," Madeline repeated disbelievingly. "He can eat ham and grits after consuming that huge supper last night?"

Celia chuckled. "Jake can eat anytime." She motioned Madeline toward the door. "You'd better hurry and dress. Knowing Jake, he'll be over here after you if you don't appear soon."

"But—but I was going to have breakfast with you," she said helplessly.

Celia tapped her foot impatiently. "Don't be silly. I'll be leaving for work in a few minutes, anyway. Go on, be with Jake and have fun." She gave Madeline a gentle nudge out of the kitchen.

Madeline didn't argue further. She rushed upstairs to her bedroom and dressed as quickly as possible in yellow walking shorts and a matching shell top.

Jake was placing a plate of ham on the table when she entered the cabin. He looked up, smiling warmly at her, and she suddenly knew that meeting Jake was the most important thing she'd done in a long time.

The closeness she'd shared with him the night before was still there. It hadn't vanished with the light of day, Madeline was thrilled to realize.

"Good morning, Maddie," he said, an appreciative gleam in his eye as he took in her sunny appearance. "I hope you're as hungry as I am. Do you know how to cook redeye gravy?"

She went to the stove and looked into the black skillet he'd used to fry the ham. "It's been a long time, but I think I can still do it."

He walked up behind her and peered over her left shoulder. "I hope so. Those grits are going to be awfully lonesome without it."

Madeline laughed softly and reached for a spoon to scrape the ham drippings from the bottom of the skillet. "I'll try, but I won't promise it will be good."

"I trust you. Show me how to do it and next time I'll cook it for you."

She turned her head to look up at him. Since he was still peering over her shoulder, the movement brought her face very close to his. The proximity made her feel breathless, and for a moment all she could do was stare at the hard line of his lips. It would be so wonderful if he would kiss her again, so wonderful and yet so dangerous.

Madeline mentally shook herself and forced her eyes back to the skillet. "It's simple, really," she told him, trying her best not to sound like a breathy actress. "You just loosen all the drippings and add some cold water. Do you have a cup handy?"

He stepped around her and retrieved a glass measuring cup from the dish drainer. "How's this?"

"Fine," she assured him and filled it with water.

"Don't you need a fire under that?" he asked, motioning toward the burner beneath the skillet.

Madeline blushed. "I told you it had been a long time." She laughed up at him and he patted her cheek.

"I'm making you nervous," he apologized. "So don't pay any attention to me. Just act like you were cooking it at home."

Madeline laughed, for there was no way Andrew would have ever eaten redeye gravy. It was too greasy, too sinfully delicious for someone like him. "Jake, there wasn't anyone up there who ever wanted redeye gravy. I never cooked it back in Ozark."

"Their loss," he said, watching her pour the water into the skillet.

Madeline stirred slowly as the fire brought the mixture to a gentle boil. "This is really all you do," she told him. "Just let it boil down and condense."

Jake sniffed the delicious aroma as steam rose from the skillet. "Mmm. My mother used to fix this stuff. Bless her heart, she was a tiny little thing, but she ate like a horse."

"Well, this is ready, if you are," she told him several minutes later.

"If I am?" he asked, hurrying to get her a bowl for the gravy. "I've been ready since my eyes opened this morning."

He filled the bowl and carried it to the table as if it were as precious as melted gold. Madeline followed him and gasped as she looked at the table he'd already loaded with food.

"My goodness, you cooked biscuits, too!" she exclaimed. "You must be a man of many talents."

He chuckled at her words as he pulled out a chair for her to sit on. "Not at all. A bachelor isn't talented, he's just forced to learn things." He took the seat opposite her and passed her the plate of biscuits. "Do you like biscuits?"

She grimaced good-naturedly. "Like them! They're a weakness of mine. I could eat them three times a day," she admitted.

"Good," he said happily as he watched her spread butter on one of them. "I'll cook them for you tomorrow morning."

She looked up at him in surprise and noticed, not for the first time, how handsome he looked in the pale blue shirt he was wearing. It clung to his broad shoulders, and she knew if she could see beneath the material it would show strong muscles and smooth warm skin the color of honey. It would probably be just as delicious to taste, too, she thought.

The idea was more than disturbing, and she bit into her biscuit with unnecessary force. "Jake, I can't eat breakfast over here tomorrow, too," she said.

He looked at her questioningly. "Really, why?" he asked easily, as if he considered her words ridiculous.

"Well, just because. Mother—" she began.

"Celia leaves for work at this time, and I know for a fact that she rarely has more than coffee and toast in the morning."

"Even so, it—"

He reached across the table and clasped her hand in his. Madeline felt a surge of warmth rush through her at his touch.

"Maddie, darling, I hate eating breakfast alone, and there's no harm in your sharing it with me."

She tried to make light of his words. "There is if I eat like this. After a while I couldn't get through the door. Then you'd have to get another secretary."

"Never," he said, releasing her hand and winking at her. "I'd have the door facings taken off first."

She laughed and decided there was no use denying how much she enjoyed being with him. He loved life and she somehow felt that with him she would learn to enjoy it in the very same way.

After breakfast they washed the dishes and left the cabin. The sun was already growing hot. It warmed Madeline's arms and shoulders as she waited for Jake to fish the motorcycle key from his pocket.

She wasn't going to try to talk him out of taking the motorcycle this time. In fact, she was secretly looking forward to holding on to his waist and feeling the wind in her face.

He put her pen and notepad in one of the sidesaddles and started the motor before Madeline climbed on behind him. In a matter of seconds they were down the driveway and heading south on Second Street.

It was a beautiful spring day. As they cruised along the street they saw several people out working in their lawns. One gray-haired man waved familiarly at Madeline, and she waved back to him.

"Who was that?" Jake asked.

"Herbert, a very old friend," she told him. "When I was small he always bought three boxes of Girl Scout cookies from me. He liked my red hair, he'd always say."

"I'll bet he'd like more than your red hair now," Jake teased.

She pinched him in the ribs and could feel his laughter even though she couldn't hear it over the sound of the motorcycle.

Jake turned west on College Avenue when they reached an intersection. Madeline felt several curious stares at them as they arrived at the campus and Jake parked beneath a huge oak.

Madeline smoothed her hair with her fingers as best she could while he fetched her notepad and pen from the saddlebag.

The spring semester was not yet over, and the campus was filled with young people strolling to and from classes. Madeline felt very out of place and conspicuous as she and Jake walked up the path toward the library.

"I graduated from here," she told him proudly. "But being here now feels like being on foreign soil."

His arm rested lightly at the back of her waist as he glanced down at her. "Don't you ever visit the campus?" he asked.

She shook her head. "Not in a long time."

For a moment he stopped upon the lush green grass. It forced her to stop also, and she looked expectantly at him.

"It seems to me there are a lot of things you haven't done in a long time," he said.

She smiled regretfully as she looked into his eyes. "Yes, I guess you're right."

Unexpectedly, his expression grew serious. "Are you going to let me do something about changing all of that?" he asked.

"I think you already are," she admitted.

He smiled at her words and began to lead her toward the library. "Now remember, Maddie. Once we get in here, I don't want any giggling or flirting," he told her in mock seriousness. "We've got to work; you've got to get all the details about Fort Claiborne today. You can't be thinking about me."

Even though she tried to prevent it, a smile tilted the corners of her mouth. "Absolutely no flirting," she promised solemnly, crossing her heart with her forefinger.

Jake didn't stop laughing until they entered the library.

That day a routine began for Madeline that would continue for weeks. Each morning she rose early, dressed, waved goodbye to her mother, then hurried to the cabin to share breakfast with Jake.

Sometimes he already had it cooked. Sometimes she helped him prepare something. After they finished eating they would go over the work they had accomplished the day before, then decide what they would do with the day ahead.

The neighbors on Amulet and Second Streets had grown accustomed to the sight of Jake ripping through the streets on his motorcycle with Madeline perched behind him.

Jake was finding the college a gold mine of historical information. The library there contained all kinds of photos, documents and other materials that traced the area's history. There was also a museum, not to mention St. Nicholas School, which was a one-room schoolhouse on the campus that had been preserved exactly as it had been in the previous century.

Jake tried to absorb all the information he could as they explored these places, but as he had told Madeline, there were just too many details to make that possible, especially since his novel planned to cover many years.

Madeline's shorthand was improving with every passing day. She was usually surprised to find almost half a notebook filled whenever they got back to the cabin. She was also surprised to find that Jake could tune out the sound of her typing and was able to concentrate on his writing.

Several days after she began helping him, Madeline suggested that she use her mother's typewriter back in the big house so that Jake could work in peace. He rejected the idea completely.

"I like you working by my side. You don't distract me; you give me inspiration," he told her.

So, Madeline stayed in the cabin with him and tried to work as quietly as she could. Yet she had to admit her favorite times were when Jake turned away from his computer and talked to her. It didn't matter if he was discussing Louisiana history or a current world event. Madeline loved to talk to him about anything. She loved being with him, watching him as, lost in thought, he worked at the computer. She loved the way his dark hair fell across his forehead and the way he smiled at her whenever he caught her looking at him.

For the first time in a long, long time Madeline was happy with what she was doing. The dress shop she had once thought so important was now pushed to the back of her thoughts. She was taking her mother's advice. There would be plenty of time for that in the future, and right now she was enjoying being with Jake.

He was like no one she had ever known, and he filled her heart with sweet joy. Each day she awoke eagerly anticipating seeing him again. Everything around her seemed beautiful and important; even the food she ate tasted wonderful.

She was in love. In spite of her haunting past, in spite of the danger the future might hold, she was in love with Jake Hunter.

"Maddie, are you ready for a bite to eat?" Jake asked, glancing at his watch one day. "It's almost twelve. The plantations will be opening around one."

"If you are," she agreed, pulling a sheet of paper from the typewriter. "Let me get these pages together and I'll be ready."

Jake watched her from across the room as she shuffled the papers around. Her full-skirted pink and green dress swished and rustled every time she moved, and several times already he had caught himself watching the way the folds caressed her shapely calves.

Although he loved having her near to him for so much of the time Jake had to admit it was also rather difficult. Her presence was, among other things, an aphrodisiac, and he was constantly tempted to touch her, hold her, feel her soft curves yield to his hands. But the night they had danced, he had decided to tread lightly, and he was determined to stick with his decision.

As the days turned into weeks she began to change; he could see it. The smiles that had so rarely lighted her face when she first arrived came much more often now. She laughed and talked freely with him and the defeated look had disappeared from her eyes. He didn't want to risk losing all of that by trying to make love to her. But Lord, this slow going was killing him! He was constantly remembering how it had been that first night when they had exchanged those few passionate kisses. He wanted it to be like that again, like that and so much more.

"I thought we might as well grab a hamburger on the way to the plantations," he suggested, rising from his seat.

Madeline reached for her notepad and purse. "Sounds good to me. If we eat fast we can be there by one or so."

The two of them were planning to explore some of the famous plantations situated south of the city. Madeline had visited them with her mother years before. But she had been merely a child then, her mind not ready to understand all the folklore associated with the places or to envision their past grandeur. She was excited about seeing them with Jake. He made everything new and exciting for her.

Jake drove them across the river and to a fast-food restaurant in the business district. Madeline had quickly learned that he was far from a health-food fanatic. He loved things that were loaded with calories, carbohydrates and all those other nasty, tempting things.

He insisted that one of the main reasons he moved from New York City was that he couldn't buy Goo Goo bars anywhere in the north. It wasn't hard for her to believe that. Not after he had practically pulled her from Maria's because his chocolates were melting! Yet what amazed Madeline about the whole thing was that he seemed the epitome of good health; his body was hard and fit. Andrew had been a stickler about food. He wouldn't have been caught dead in a fast-food place. However, Andrew's body couldn't compare with Jake's. And Andrew was at least six years younger! So much for the health-food wave of the eighties, Madeline thought as she watched Jake make short work of a stack of French fries smothered with catsup.

"What is amusing you now?" Jake asked, glancing up at her while reaching for his cola.

"Who says I'm amused?"

"Maddie, I saw that secretive little smile on your lips. You do that quite often, you know."

She took a bite of hamburger, chewed it, then swallowed before she said, "You just happen to do things that amuse me."

"That's great to know." He chuckled. "The lady constantly laughs at me behind my back."

"That's not what I meant, Jake," she told him. "I meant that you're nothing like I would expect an author to be—" He grinned, and she went on. "You're nothing like—the men I've been around, either."

"You mean, I'm nothing like your ex-husband, don't you?" he said suddenly.

Madeline stiffened at the mention of Andrew. "No, you're nothing like him," she answered in a low voice.

His keen gray eyes inspected her suddenly guarded expression. He didn't like to think the man in her past could still have any real effect on her, but it was obvious she was not completely over her failed marriage. "Tell me about him, Maddie. What was he like?"

She shook her head. "You wouldn't want to know. You wouldn't like Andrew. He's not your kind of person at all."

"Why?" he prompted, encouraged that she had opened up even this much.

Her gaze dropped to the tabletop, as if it was easier to speak while not looking at Jake. "Andrew is a conservative type, very conventional, very career- and business-minded. His ambition is work, not enjoyment. He believes in perfection and has little time for anyone who isn't perfect."

"Lord, Maddie! I hope you're exaggerating," he said with disgust.

Her smile was full of mockery. "If anything, I'm understating the case."

"What did you see in him? What kept you with him for so long?"

Madeline didn't want to answer those questions. She had no feeling left for Andrew. He had slowly destroyed any love she had felt for him. Why she had married Andrew no longer even mattered to her.

"I was twenty-one, Jake. There were stars in my eyes. All I saw then was a handsome young man and a new and different life. But I woke up," she added cynically. "I woke up with a jolt."

He continued to study her thoughtfully. "And you stayed because you hate to fail. Or were you just trying to become that model of perfection your husband wanted?"

Madeline stabbed a French fry with her plastic fork. She had to end this conversation. She couldn't let Jake keep chipping away at her protective armor. If he did, he would come to see just how flawed she really was.

"Maybe," she conceded. "Because when we both finally admitted I'd never be the perfect wife, we ended it."

He swallowed the last of his hamburger, then took both her hands in his. Madeline watched him in confusion as he stared intently at them. When he finished his inspection he reached for her chin and turned her head to the left and then to the right. He studied her face, her throat, her shoulders and even the provocative shape of her breast until Madeline turned red with embarrassment.

"Jake! What are you doing?" she demanded beneath her breath. "The people in here are going to think we're both crazy!"

He shrugged and grinned as though that possibility didn't bother him in the least. "I'm looking for all those cracks and flaws. I can't find any."

Madeline began to wad up the paper containers in which their food had been served. "Jake, do you know what some Southerners would call you?" she groaned. "Tetched." She reached over and touched his forehead to stress her point. "Tetched in the head."

Laughing, he took her hand again and pulled her up from the tiny table. "Come on, dear Maddie, we've got a short way to go but a lot of things to see."

Outside it was muggy, and low-hanging clouds were beginning to cover the sky. Madeline looked up at them despairingly.

"I should have brought my umbrella along. It looks as if it's going to pour."

"I'll go ahead and put the top up if you want," Jake said as they reached the Cadillac.

"Oh, let's leave it. Maybe we'll be lucky and the rain will go around us," she suggested.

As they drove south on Highway 1 they passed a host of preserved antebellum plantations lining the Cane River. Although many were magnificent they decided to continue until they found the famous Melrose plantation.

Melrose was steeped in the romantic past. There were eight structures on the grounds, including the breathtaking main house.

Jake was interested in the later owners of the plantation. The couple had been big patrons of the arts, and many famous artists and authors had been invited to live and work at Melrose. Such famous writers as Faulkner, Steinbeck, and Erskine Caldwell were among those that had stayed there.

Madeline wondered if it inspired Jake to walk through the same rooms those brilliant authors had lived and worked in. She could have told him that it was an inspiration for her to be able to see it all with him, especially when Jake held her hand or put his arm around her waist as they strolled in the deep shade of the oaks and cypress trees.

Later that evening they went to the Bayou Folk Museum. It finally started to rain just as they completed their tour and they decided to make a run for the Cadillac.

By the time they slid onto the car's wet seats the rain was pouring down. Jake was laughing so hard he didn't even try to put the top up on the car. He just looked at Madeline and laughed as sheets of water continued to soak them.

Desperate, Madeline began banging him over the head with her notepad. "You idiot," she cried frantically, "We're getting drenched! Do something!"

"Okay! Okay!" he said, his laughter finally dying down. "I'm trying."

Finally the top began to move up and over their heads. Once it was stretched into place the rain drummed against the vinyl with fierce determination.

Madeline looked down at her saturated dress, and then at Jake. His tropical shirt was stuck to his chest and shoulders, and rivulets of water were running from his hair onto his face.

The car's interior wasn't in much better condition. Water was everywhere, on the dash, the floorboard, the seats and armrests. She looked around despairingly for a place to put her soggy notepad.

"Try the glove compartment," Jake suggested.

Madeline cast him a dismal grin. "You really are insane. Look at us! Just look!"

He turned in the seat to examine her saturated clothes and red hair, which was now plastered against her scalp. At the sight of her pathetic condition, a helpless fit of laughter struck him again.

"I've never seen a drowned red rat before," he said between gales of laughter.

Infuriated, Madeline raised her notepad threateningly.

"You crazy man! You did this to me and you sit there and have the nerve to call me a red rat!"

His laughter was so infectious that Madeline could not keep from giggling herself. She knew she looked ridiculous, but so did he!

After a moment Jake reached out, grabbed her, and pulled her to him. Their wet faces were separated by mere inches.

They both grew motionless, their eyes meeting.

"You're not a rat," he murmured, smiling softly. "You're a water nymph."

His voice had slipped to a dangerous whisper and Madeline felt the sexual tension between them increase until she was a little bit frightened.

"Oh, Jake."

It was all she could say and Jake's face moved even closer. He reached up and pushed back the wet tendrils of hair from her face.

"Kiss me, Maddie. Kiss me."

His warm breath fanned across her cheeks, feeling like a seductive caress. It was impossible to think about consequences when his very nearness was drugging her, his gray eyes beckoning to her, urging her on.

She felt herself inching toward him and knew there was no more thinking to be done. It was all feeling as Jake's lips met hers.

Madeline's arms moved around his neck. Her fingers pressed against his wet shirt and felt the warm hard muscles beneath the sodden fabric. She was experiencing that same abandonment in his arms that she had the first time they had kissed. That same sweet ache was building inside her.

When the tip of her tongue pushed brazenly between his lips Jake responded by capturing it between his sharp white teeth. Madeline shuddered at the intimate contact while Jake made a guttural sound of pleasure. She had the sensation of falling, then realized they had slid down onto the wet seat.

Outside the rain drummed with continued ferocity, matching the rising desire between them. Madeline's fingers pushed into his wet, dark hair and pressed against his scalp. This was Jake, the man she had come to desire more than anything in the world.

Involuntarily, her body shifted against him so that her breasts were crushed against his chest.

Jake fumbled with the buttons on her bodice, then in an instant his mouth was on her breast. Her nipples were like

NO COST! NO OBLIGATION! NO PURCHASE NECESSARY!

PLAY "LUCKY 7"
AND GET AS MANY AS SIX FREE GIFTS...

HOW TO PLAY:

1. With a coin, carefully scratch off the three silver boxes at the right. This makes you eligible to receive one or more free books, and possibly other gifts, depending on what is revealed beneath the scratch-off area.

2. You'll receive brand-new Silhouette Romance® novels, never before published. When you return this card, we'll send you the books and gifts you qualify for *absolutely free*.

3. And, a month later, we'll send you 6 additional novels to read and enjoy. If you decide to keep them, you'll pay only $1.95 per book. And $1.95 per book is all you pay. There is no charge for shipping and handling. There are no hidden extras.

4. We'll also send you additional free gifts from time to time, as well as our monthly newsletter.

5. You must be completely satisfied, or you may return a

honey to him, and he didn't know whether it was Madeline or himself who was moaning in sweet torment. He only knew he had to have her. He didn't care where they were. All he could think was how sweet it would be to make love to her, until he was weak and breathless.

As if they had a will of their own, his hands slid beneath the wet folds of her skirt. Her thighs were damp and soft, and his fingers trembled as they slipped over the lacy waistband of her panties. He was certain he was going out of his mind, and that Maddie was going along with him.

Suddenly Madeline was resisting beneath him, striving to push him away. It took Jake's confused senses a moment to recognize and understand her responses. When he did, he looked down at her uncomprehendingly. Her cheeks were wet, and he didn't know if it was from rain or tears.

"Maddie—what's wrong? Are you crying—why?"

She shook her head and this time he could actually see the tears forming in her eyes. With a regretful sigh he eased away from her and she quickly scrambled to a sitting position.

Her downcast face was hidden by her wet hair as she said bleakly, "I can't make love to you, Jake."

He stared at her in confusion. She had wanted him; he knew it, had felt it. Why was she doing this to him, to both of them!

"Madeline, what are you saying? You want me as much as I want you!"

"Yes," she answered simply, finally lifting her face to look at him.

Jake wanted to be furious with her. He wanted to, but he couldn't. Not once he saw that heartsick, defeated expression in her eyes. My God, how he loved her! Couldn't she see it?

"Then don't play games with me, Madeline."

She shook her head, her eyes imploring him to understand. "I'm not, Jake—I—" She moved closer to him and reached up, her hands tenderly framing his face. "I told you before, you don't know me. Not really," she added as she watched him frown impatiently. "But that's beside the point. I guess I'm just old-fashioned. I don't think I could have sex with you, or any man unless I were married to him. I'm just that kind of a woman."

He laughed, a deep rich sound. "That's easy enough to settle. We'll just get married."

Madeline stared at him in disbelief. She swiftly pulled away from him and turned her face toward the window, but all she could see was steam fogging up the glass and rain pelting against the windshield. "I—you're crazy! I'll never marry again. And you don't want to marry me—not really."

In less than a second he moved across the seat and grasped her by the shoulders. "For the first time in my life I know that I do want to marry," he said, his cheek pressed against the curve of her neck. "For the first time I've found the woman I want to share the rest of my life with. I know it sounds ridiculous to say these things since we barely know each other, but trust me, Maddie."

The intense conviction of his words caused her to clench her fingers into a tight little fist. Oh, how she wanted to turn and kiss him madly, to tell him she wanted nothing more than to be his wife. But she couldn't! She would be cheating him. And she loved him too much to do that.

"I—I told you, Jake. I'll never marry again. Never! Never!"

"Madeline," he began, but by now she was actually sobbing.

"Take me home, Jake. Please, just take me home."

He touched her hair with longing and regret. It was an effort to make himself move away from her, to slide across the seat and start the Cadillac. But he did.

After the motor was running, he turned on the wipers and waited for them to clear the windshield. Yet they couldn't wipe the vision of Madeline's face from his mind, or the misery he had seen etched upon it.

Chapter Seven

Dressed in jeans and an oversize shirt, Madeline was staring pensively out the French doors in her bedroom when the telephone rang.

Reluctantly, she crossed to the bedside table and picked up the receiver.

"Madeline?"

At the sound of Jake's voice she gripped the handle of the receiver so tightly her hand began to hurt. She couldn't believe he would want to talk to her after what had happened that afternoon in the car.

"Maddie, are you there?" he asked.

"Yes, I'm here," she answered huskily.

"I—will you come down to the cabin? We need to talk."

Madeline began to tremble, that same cold, uncontrollable trembling she had experienced on their silent drive back home. "No—I don't think I should. It won't—"

"Maddie—darling, please," he implored, his words

melting Madeline's heart. "I have something to tell you and it's—it's not just about this afternoon."

Madeline stared helplessly around the bedroom. She would have to give in and talk to him. If she didn't he would probably just come to the house and search her out.

"Okay." She sighed heavily. "I'll be over in a minute or two."

After hanging up the phone Madeline walked to the closet and searched out an old umbrella. It was still raining, and she didn't relish the idea of getting wet a second time.

Before she left the bedroom she looked in the mirror. The rain had washed away all her makeup, making her face seem a white oval compared to the bright turquoise of her blouse. She had pulled her wet hair back into a single braid, and she realized that she looked very young and vulnerable in spite of her twenty-eight years.

Minutes later Jake held the door to the cabin open for her. She closed the umbrella and shook the water from it before stepping from the little porch and over the threshold.

"I'm glad you decided to come," he said, his back to her as he walked to the breakfast bar. "I've just made some coffee—like some?"

"Yes," she murmured and crossed the room.

She was sitting stiffly on the edge of the couch when he turned to look at her, one brow arched as he held up a bottle of apricot brandy. "Brandy?"

"Why not?" she replied, after an instant's hesitation. Maybe it would warm the chill that had crept over her and make speaking to Jake a little easier.

He splashed some of the brandy into both cups then carried them across the room. Madeline noticed he had changed into a dry pair of jeans and one of those sleeveless white undershirts that men had worn seemingly since time began. The cutout arms and neck exposed the heavy muscles of his arms and shoulders. She could see the shape of his nipples beneath the thin ribbed material and the dark hair that grew between them.

"Here you go," he told her. Handing her the cup, he joined her on the couch.

"Thank you," she said, trying not to notice that he had left only a small space between them. She was still quaking with the memory of being in his arms. Was he trying to remind her of it all over again?

"Actually, I wanted to let you know I received a phone call shortly after we arrived home."

Madeline swallowed some of the brandy and coffee, hoping it would calm her, hoping it would block out the insatiable longing she felt for this man.

"Oh? Something important?" she asked stiffly.

"Yes. As a matter of fact, it was."

He brought his cup to his lips and Madeline watched as he drank a few swallows and wondered how this news could possibly affect her.

"It was William Black."

For a moment her expression was blank. "You mean William Black, the film producer?" she finally asked.

He nodded. "Yes, you see, he's producing a movie from my novel, *The Legacy*."

Madeline was shocked, to say the least. He'd never mentioned any of this before. "I would never have known it from your behavior. I would think you'd be shouting it from the rafters," she told him.

He shrugged as though it was no big deal and rose from the couch to stroll restlessly around the living area. "I'm not that turned on by movies. Don't get me wrong; the money is great. But another of my novels was turned into a movie and I was very disappointed. They ripped into the plot until it was just a vague image of the characters and story I'd created."

"Then why are you allowing them to produce this one?"

He took another swallow of the coffee, then looked directly at her. "Because I told them the only way they could have the rights was to let me help write the script."

Madeline's mind began racing ahead, and she realized he was trying to tell her that sooner or later he'd be leaving Natchitoches, that he'd be getting on with his life in other places, with other people. How could she stand it? For a moment she thought she wouldn't want to live if she couldn't have his happy, handsome face always near.

"So, what does this mean? Why are you telling me this?" she asked quietly.

Both her hands were cupped around the warm mug. She lifted it to her lips and drank. Right now she wanted the alcohol in her system; she needed it to numb the effects his words were bound to cause.

"Because I've got to fly to Miami tomorrow. If you read the book, you'll know it takes place in the Keys and they're shooting nearly all of it on location."

"You—you mean you haven't finished the script yet?" she asked in disbelief.

He shook his head. "We finished the script a few months ago. But William and the director think that the final couple of scenes aren't working properly. He wants me to meet with the other two writers who are already on the set and do some revising."

Madeline swallowed convulsively. He was leaving. She felt shattered and frightened. "How—how long will you be gone?"

"A week. Maybe two. Depends on how the script goes."

Two weeks! It would seem like an eternity without him. "I—suppose you'll be taking Mr. Miles with you," she said quietly.

He glanced at the cat, who was curled up asleep in a corner. "No, I thought I'd ask Celia to take care of him while I'm away."

Madeline looked at him questioningly. Why wasn't he asking her to do it? She was the one who had fondled and spoiled the cat every day. Was he that bitter toward her now?

So, Mr. Miles, she silently mused, it looks like he's deserting us both. She felt dead inside.

Jake placed his coffee cup on the dining table and crossed to Madeline. Surprise held her motionless as he squatted down before her and took both her hands in his.

"I want you to go with me, Maddie." He spoke the words feverishly in his eagerness to persuade her. "We can get married in Miami and spend our honeymoon in the Keys. The script won't keep me tied up for long. It will be wonderful. We'll charter a boat and play in the ocean and make ourselves sick on Key lime pie."

Madeline's head swam. She couldn't believe he was once again saying he wanted to marry her! She couldn't believe how much she wanted to cry yes!

She clenched his hand tightly in hers. "Jake, didn't you hear me earlier? I'm not going to marry again."

"I heard you. But that's all I heard. No reasons, no explanations. I can't accept that, Madeline. I love you too much."

"You—you love me?" Her voice was barely audible. She had never expected to hear him say those words. She knew he was sexually attracted to her, that he enjoyed her company, but she had never guessed that he could love her.

"Is the idea that incredible to you?" he asked. "I thought you could read it all over me. I thought I said it every time I looked at you."

Madeline shook her head. "No—you can't."

"Says who?" he demanded. "Your ex-husband? Well, Maddie, I'm not looking for a perfect woman. I'm looking for the woman who's perfect for me. You just happen to be her."

Madeline could stand it no longer. She couldn't think clearly so close to Jake. She pulled away from him and nearly ran across the room.

Outside, the rain was still falling heavily, and the cabin felt like a warm, safe cocoon. It seemed that in the whole universe there was only this quiet little room, Jake and herself. It would be so easy to forget the outside world, so easy to let him make slow, delicious love to her.

But she had to keep her senses about her. Above all else, she couldn't give in to him. He meant too much to her. God, what was she going to do?

With her back to him she stared out the window at the falling rain. Magnolia blossoms adorned the tree limbs just a few feet away from the cabin. Drops of water splashed off their waxy white petals and Madeline knew the sweet scent of them would be heavy in the damp air.

"Don't do this to me, Jake," she begged. "Don't pry me open so that you can see all the ugly things inside—things that I don't want you to see."

Within seconds he was behind her, his arms around her waist. His voice was sweet and husky in her ear.

"Madeline, you don't understand. I don't care what happened in your past. I don't care if there were ugly things between you and your ex-husband. And even if you told me you were guilty of having an affair, it couldn't change my feelings. Nothing, absolutely nothing could do that."

How could he know that, she wondered despairingly. She swallowed and blinked in an effort to ward off the tears that were burning her eyes.

When she had first learned she could never bear children, she had been overwhelmed with disappointment. But those feelings seemed very mild compared with the devastation she was experiencing now. To marry Jake and give him a child, to produce a baby from their love, would be the greatest thing she could imagine. And to know that she couldn't was shattering her heart into a million pieces.

She turned in his arms and lifted her hands to rest them upon his chest. Moisture shone in her green eyes as she looked up at him.

"You might say that now. But later—later I know you'd regret marrying me."

The love she saw in his eyes was swiftly replaced by impatience and he gave her a little shake.

"You're not making sense, Madeline. And I'm not going to let you out of this cabin until you do. I want you to tell me what you're so determined to hide. What is this thing that's made you feel so useless and defeated? Tell me, Maddie, tell me!"

His harsh words pierced her heart. She stared at him looking wild and wounded.

"I can't," she cried.

Desperate anger overwhelmed him. His fingers clamped down hard on her shoulders, and he pulled her toward him until her face was within an inch of his.

"You can and you will! I won't go to the Keys without you! You're not going to keep tormenting both of us like this!"

Tears began to stream down her cheeks. The sight of them twisted something deep inside him, and his mouth fastened over her trembling lips with hungry desperation. In spite of the pain she felt Madeline responded to him and in a matter of seconds she could think of nothing but the kiss.

Both of them were breathing hard when their lips parted and when Madeline looked into his gray eyes she knew there wasn't anywhere else to run.

She drew a ragged breath, then the words came tumbling out. "I can't have children, Jake. I can conceive, but I can't carry them past two or three months. So—I—I could never give you a child."

She dropped her head in despair and Jake looked down at her with incredulity. He felt shocked and greatly disappointed, but at the same time he was relieved.

"I—I had two miscarriages during my marriage to Andrew. After the last one, tests concluded I had a genetic defect. It doesn't affect me in any way—but it makes me incapable of carrying a child to full term. It's impossible—it's—oh, Jake," she choked out painfully.

"Maddie—my darling, my baby. That's not anything to feel ashamed or guilty of. And it's all right. It's all right, I tell you."

She clung tightly to him. "You say that now, but you can't possibly know that you wouldn't regret it later on. And I don't ever want to see that cold, accusing look on your face that I saw on Andrew's. It—it would kill me if I ever saw it on you!"

"Oh, Madeline," he groaned. "I won't lie to you. It does disappoint me to think that we could never have a child together. It hurts me, because I know it hurts you. But that doesn't mean I'm going to suddenly stop loving you. You can't simply turn love on and off like a machine."

Madeline sighed and wiped her eyes. She felt old and exhausted. "Then go to the Keys and think about it. Think about what you'd be getting and what you'd be giving up. And—and one way or the other, I'll be here when you return."

He shook his head in protest. "I don't want to go without you."

"You're going to have to," she insisted quietly. "Because I'm not going, and you have to finish the script. Besides," she added, "you'll see things differently when you're away from me. It—it will be good for both of us."

"You're not leaving me any alternatives, are you?" he demanded.

Seeing her shake her head, he sighed and said, "Well, I'll go and I'll think. But it won't change anything, Maddie, nothing at all. I love you now, I'll love you when I get back, I'll love you forever."

He kissed her then, and Madeline closed her eyes and met his lips with a yearning she couldn't hide.

In her heart she prayed that his words would remain true.

Madeline had supper cooked and waiting for her mother when she arrived home from work. She had forced herself to prepare the meal, hoping the task would help take her mind off Jake.

So far it had failed miserably. Her mind was consumed with thoughts of him and she was unable to concentrate on her mother's bubbly chatter.

"Everyone is excited about the dress shop. All the women at work have promised to buy from you," Celia said as they ate dessert.

Madeline had prepared strawberry shortcake, one of her favorite desserts, but tonight it might as well have been cardboard for all the enjoyment she was getting from it.

"That's very nice," she said absently.

"You didn't get any word from Andrew today, did you? It won't be long until the building is vacated. You're going to have to make up your mind about the loan. I'm just glad you decided to take the three-year lease. I don't think you'll regret it at all."

"I hope you're right," Madeline said glumly. "It took nearly all of my savings. I'm beginning to think Andrew is dragging his feet. He's probably decided to rent the house out to someone and keep the cash for himself and tell m that it hasn't sold because the market is bad. It would be just like him.''

Celia put down her spoon and looked thoughtfully at her daughter. ''Well, I for one think you should make a trip up there and see for yourself. You know he's a swine, Madeline. I wouldn't put anything past him.''

''Money or no money,'' Madeline told her mother, ''I'm not making a trip up to Ozark. Not now.'' There were too many far more important things on her mind. She didn't care about the money, and as far as the dress shop went, she wouldn't be able to put her heart into it unless Jake was there to share it all with her.

Celia got up to fetch the coffeepot. ''By the way, why isn't Jake having supper with us? It's so gloomy. I wish he would come over. Rain depresses me and Jake always livens things up.''

Madeline poked at the strawberries in her bowl. ''Jake is packing. He won't be over tonight.''

Celia stared at her daughter in total surprise. ''Packing? But where is he going?''

Madeline tried to sound indifferent, but it was very hard to do when tears were blurring her vision. ''He's flying down to the Keys. They're filming *The Legacy*, and he has to do a little revision on the script.''

''Oh well, that should be exciting! But I'll hate having him away.'' She looked at Madeline and smiled. ''I guess I've grown attached to him living right here by us and cheering up this quiet house.''

''Yes—I have, too.'' Madeline rose swiftly from the table. ''Mother, if you don't mind I think I'll lie down for a while. It's—been a long day.''

''Of course, darling,'' Celia said, looking from her daughter's uneaten dessert to her pale face. ''You're not ill, are you?''

''No. I'm just tired.''

Celia turned her attention back to the strawberries. "If you're sure you'll be okay, I think I'll drive down to Charles's and get him going with a game of cards."

"Yes. Go ahead," Madeline urged. "Charles will be glad to see you."

After her mother had left, Madeline lay on her four-poster and listened to the rain fall. She wished for anything to take her mind off Jake.

Several times she walked over to the windows and looked down at his cabin. His lights were still on and it was all she could do to keep from going down the stairs and out the back to his door.

Yet seeing him again would be useless. She had already said everything she could say, and she knew she had to stick to her convictions. If she agreed to marry Jake now, without giving him the time to think it over, it would be doing them both an injustice.

Her failed marriage to Andrew had been bad enough. To have Jake and then lose him would be more than her heart could endure.

By the next morning the rain had stopped, but the sky was still covered with heavy gray clouds. They matched Madeline's mood as she dressed in a white gauze dress.

Jake was leaving in a half hour, and she had promised to drive him to the airport since he didn't want to leave the Cadillac parked there. She wasn't looking forward to saying goodbye to him. In fact, she didn't know how she was going to get through it without breaking down and making a fool of herself.

It seemed incredible that it had been only a matter of weeks since she had driven into Natchitoches that first day and Jake had tried to pick her up on his motorcycle. How could she ever have guessed he would come to mean so much to her, that he would turn her feelings and her life around so drastically?

The question reminded her that there was a force up in the heavens mapping out their lives below. And at the moment she was praying that the map would lead her back into Jake's arms. Miracles did happen, and she needed one badly.

Jake was piling his suitcases into the back seat of the car when Madeline walked out to the driveway. His usual jeans and casual shirt had been replaced by slacks and an expensive-looking tailored shirt.

"Good morning," she said as she reached the car.

He turned to see her standing just behind him, a white purse clutched tightly in her hands.

"I see you didn't change your mind and bring your suitcases along with you," he said with obvious disappointment.

Madeline shook her head. "No, I didn't."

He moved a step closer and placed his hand over hers. "I won't try to change your mind now, Maddie," he said quietly. "But I will tell you it's killing me to leave you like this." He smiled ruefully. "I'm leaving for a couple of weeks and it's wringing my heart. I've never known a woman I wanted to be around for more than twenty-four hours. Now I've found one I don't even want to be away from for twenty-four minutes."

Madeline tried to smile. "You'll be busy with the movie. And with you down there, I know it will be a big success."

He glanced at his watch. "I hate to say it, but I think we should be going. I'm sure the pilot will have the plane ready."

Jake drove them down through town and out to the airport. All through the short trip Madeline kept stealing glances at him, and every time she did her heart gave a painful little contraction.

He was handsome, sexy and successful. No doubt women had always looked at him and wanted him. No doubt there would be women down in the Keys who would find him fascinating, too.

No, don't worry about other women, she admonished herself. But there would be parties, movie stars—warm ocean breezes—

Trying to dispel the vision of Jake in the arms of another woman, Madeline said, "I'm going to miss you, Jake. You know that, don't you?"

He sighed as he parked the Cadillac. "Yes, I know it, Maddie. And I know that in your heart you believe you're doing the right thing."

He turned off the motor and moved closer to her. His cologne wafted around her, and she thought he looked suave and sophisticated, nothing at all like the crazy guy who had driven her around on his Harley-Davidson and dared her to kiss him while they waited for the traffic light to change color.

"But I can tell you right now, Maddie," he said. "I won't change my mind. I won't change my feelings. All this separation is going to do is waste precious time we could have shared."

He reached for her hands and clutched them tightly. "I'll never take anything for granted, Jake. Especially not my happiness or yours."

"If those words are supposed to comfort me, they don't," he said. "But I guess right now they're all I have."

Sighing with reluctance, he got out of the car and began to pull his suitcases out of the back seat and set them on the ground. Madeline climbed out of the car and followed him around to the other side.

Off in the distance she noticed a man checking over a red and white Cessna. She supposed it was the one Jake had chartered.

"It looks like the pilot is about ready. I should be going," he said.

Madeline nodded and tried to smile brightly. It was one of the hardest things she'd ever done. "Have—have a safe trip," she told him huskily, "and I'll see you when you get back."

She didn't protest when he took her into his arms. In truth, she welcomed it desperately. Tears burned her eyes and throat as she clung tightly to his strong shoulders.

He looked down into her face, a wry grin tugging at his lips. "You know," he whispered roughly, "you look damn sexy in white." His fingers slid under the tiny collar of her dress and touched the soft skin beneath it.

Tears gathered in Madeline's eyes. "I love you, Jake—love you desperately."

Her words touched him so deeply that he was unable to speak. Instead he kissed her hard on the mouth, then grabbed his cases and headed across the parking area.

He turned once and saw she was still standing beside the Cadillac. He waved to her and she waved back. For once in his life Jake wished he weren't a famous author who was forced to make business trips. He wished he were just some guy who drove a dump truck or pushed cows. He wished he could have met Madeline long ago and married her when she'd been eighteen, long before pain had ever crossed her path.

Madeline waited beside the car until Jake and his cases were loaded into the Cessna. Soon it began to taxi down the runway. Madeline watched it pick up speed, then finally lift from the ground. As it banked into a curve and climbed upward toward the ceiling of gray clouds, she felt as if her very life was on that plane.

Chapter Eight

The clouds completely disappeared, letting the hot Louisiana sun beat down unmercifully. All the moisture that had fallen the day and night before made the humidity almost unendurable. Steam rose up from the wet ground, sapping the energy from anyone who went out-of-doors.

Madeline spent most of the day in the house under the air conditioner. After Jake had gone she had let Mr. Miles into the big house with her. He had followed her around all morning, rubbing against her legs and emitting pathetically soulful cries.

She suspected he missed Jake. He had always taken Mr. Miles with him, so the cat must be feeling as deserted as she did.

Madeline opened an expensive can of salmon and gave it to the cat. Celia wouldn't be too happy about the fish, but Madeline couldn't help it. She felt sorry for the tomcat and even sorrier for herself.

She knew that she should be using this time to plan her dress shop. She still needed to make a budget and decide what sort of inventory she could start with. There were a dozen other things she needed to consider, but she just couldn't keep her mind on the project.

You should have gone with him, an accusing voice repeated in her head. You could be there now with him, as his wife. You could be happy and enjoy the present.

The voice went on and on until Madeline was certain she was going insane. She switched off the television with a vengeance, reached for the telephone and dialed her mother's work number.

"Celia Beaumont, please," she said when someone answered the phone.

After a few moments there was another ring, then Celia answered.

"Mother, are you busy?"

"Madeline, how nice!" Celia exclaimed. "What are you doing?"

"I'm not doing anything," she answered truthfully. "Have you gone to lunch yet?"

"I'll be going in about fifteen minutes. I'd love for you to join me."

"I'll meet you at the bank."

After she had hung up, Madeline ran upstairs, changed from her jeans to a bright purple dress, painted a bit of pink on her mouth and hurried downstairs. She had to get away from the house, even if only for an hour.

She decided to take Jake's Cadillac. She had become very fond of the old car, and being in it gave her a strange sense of contentment.

At the bank parking lot, she parked beside her mother's Ford and waited. When Celia appeared, she happily kissed Madeline's cheek.

"Darling, I'm so glad you called. This is very nice."

She started to unlock the Ford, but Madeline said, "Don't bother with that, we'll take my—I mean, Jake's car."

Celia didn't argue or mention the slip of Madeline's tongue. "I must say, I miss Jake but if it's going to give me a little time with my daughter, I can't gripe."

Madeline didn't say anything. Instead she asked, "Where shall we go? Someplace nice, or someplace fast?"

She started the motor and began to back out of the parking space.

Celia said, "There's a good pizza place just around the corner. They have delicious salads. Good spaghetti, too."

"Good, we'll go there."

In just a matter of minutes they were sitting in a cool, dark booth, giving a waitress their orders.

"So, have you been busy giving loans today?" Madeline asked her mother after the waitress left. She stirred sugar into her tea and leaned back in her seat.

"Very busy," Celia answered. "I think everyone needs money these days."

"Amen," Madeline agreed.

"So," Celia said, "What have you been doing this morning?"

Madeline couldn't hold back her restless sigh. "Nothing! I've walked from room to room about a dozen times, started reading four different novels, and talked to Mr. Miles."

Celia smiled knowingly. "Not like following Jake around with a notepad, is it?"

Madeline shook her head. "No. Not at all. I don't know what I'm going to do for the next two weeks."

"Consider it a vacation. Go visit some of the friends you haven't seen in a long time," Celia suggested. "It would be advantageous to your business to let all your old acquaintances know you're back in town."

Madeline shrugged. "It's been so long since I've been in contact with any of them. I doubt they'd even recognize me."

Celia's dark blond brows lifted slyly as she looked over Madeline's shoulder. "Well, here comes one who will remember you," she said softly.

"Who?" Madeline asked, catching the warning note in her mother's voice.

"Rachel Connors. Remember? She was one of your best friends in college," Celia reminded her daughter.

"How could I forget the back stabber who loved to spread rumors about me?" Madeline demanded under her breath.

"Madeline Spencer as I live and breathe," the woman exclaimed.

Celia and Madeline both looked up to see Rachel standing beside their booth. Her raven-black hair was styled in a short geometric cut, and her lips and nails were painted a bright coral that clashed with her milk-white skin. She was smiling at Madeline as though she couldn't believe she was looking at the right woman.

"Hello, Rachel," Madeline said politely. "How are you?"

"I'm fine, darling, but what are you doing in Natchitoches? Did you bring Andrew this time?"

Madeline took a deep breath. "No, I didn't. And I live here now—with mother, actually."

"Oh, my Lord! You don't mean poor Andrew—that you're a widow?"

As if you would really care, Madeline thought nastily. "No, nothing like that. Andrew and I are divorced now."

Rachel stared aghast, as though Madeline's words were unbelievable. "Divorce! My dear, I would never have dreamed it of you. Your wedding was so beautiful, the picture-perfect fairy tale."

Haven't you learned by now that fairy tales never last? Madeline wanted to ask Rachel. "Yes, but we had our problems. We're both much happier now."

Rachel's expression grew coy. "To be honest," she said in a low voice, "I was always jealous of you, Maddie. You always seemed to have everything you wanted. Looks, brains, boyfriends. It was nearly impossible to compete with you."

It was Madeline's turn to be surprised. She had never dreamed that she had been thought of as the girl who had everything.

"Rachel," she half-scolded. "We were friends. I didn't think of it as competing."

"That's the only fault you ever had," she told Madeline with a savvy chuckle. "You were always too nice."

"Why don't you come over and visit us sometime, Rachel?" Celia interjected. "Madeline is planning to open a clothing store here in Natchitoches. She can tell you all about it."

Madeline frowned at her mother, but Rachel didn't notice. She was too busy digesting Celia's news.

"That's wonderful!" Rachel exclaimed. "And I will drop by, Mrs. Beaumont. I'd love to hear all about it."

Celia smiled smugly while underneath the table Madeline drummed her nails against the seat.

"You know, Maddie," Rachel went on, "I saw Janie Pendleton a few days ago, and she told me she thought you were back in town." Her smile was sugary. "She said she saw you with some gorgeous-looking man with dark hair. Well, I told her it just couldn't be you. That you were married to a thin blond." She laughed. "I just can't believe it. You divorced. I didn't think you had it in you, Madeline."

Madeline had heard just about all she could stand and opened her mouth to speak at the same moment the waitress arrived with their food. She closed her mouth and waited as the waitress placed garlic bread, bowls of salad and plates of spaghetti on the table.

At last Rachel said, "I've really got to run and let you get to your lunch. It was lovely seeing you, Maddie. Call me, won't you?"

Madeline nodded, then sighed with relief as Rachel walked away from them. "Well, I can see Rachel hasn't changed a bit. She'll head for a telephone as soon as she gets out of here."

Celia laughed as though the whole thing was amusing. "Probably. But why do you care?"

Madeline glared at her mother. "Why?" she demanded, grabbing her fork. "You know why. She'll tell everyone I'm having an affair and that I must have divorced Andrew for another man! She'll paint me as some hussy who—"

"Madeline," Celia scolded. "You're being ridiculous and far too sensitive. Everyone who really knows you knows that you're not like that."

"That's beside the point. Rachel has always loved to put me down. You remember how she started that rumor that I was sleeping with that fraternity guy. I wanted to choke her!"

Celia picked up a piece of garlic bread and rolled her eyes with amused disbelief. "My Lord, Maddie, you were practically children then, probably not more than eighteen. Can't you forget it?"

"No!" Madeline shot back.

A wry expression on her face, Celia watched Madeline sprinkle cheese over her salad and spaghetti. "You sound just like your daddy," she said wistfully. "Asa's feelings, whether they were right or wrong, were never meek and mild. You feel things with a passion, just like he did."

As Madeline poked at her salad, a reluctant smile spread over her face. It wasn't too often that Celia spoke of Asa

Beaumont and when she did it was usually to compare father and daughter.

"Yes, I guess I do feel things too deeply. One of my biggest problems I suppose," Madeline conceded.

"Well, putting Rachel aside, you shouldn't let other people's opinions worry you so. I think Andrew is partly the reason for this perfect image you want to present to everyone. And it's ridiculous! You don't know how many times I've cursed myself for allowing you to marry that—that leech."

Madeline looked at her mother with amusement. "Allow? Mother, I was twenty-one. There was hardly anything you could have done about it."

Celia chewed a piece of garlic bread. "No. You're probably right there. There's not too much a mother can do when her child doesn't do what she wants her to do."

Her child. The words pricked at Madeline. She would never be able to say my child, my son, my daughter, my baby. And if she married Jake, he would never be able to say it, either. How could she do that to him? It would be robbing him of the most precious thing a person could ever have.

Madeline swallowed a piece of tomato and looked at her mother. "You know, it surprised me to hear Rachel say she was jealous of me. I can't believe she thought of me as the girl with everything. Isn't that a laugh?"

Celia smiled to herself. "Darling, put your fork down and look at yourself. You're beautiful, intelligent, young and healthy. You've a whole wide, wonderful life ahead of you."

Madeline knew her mother was right. There were so many things she should be grateful for. But when she had left Ozark for Louisiana, things had been so different. She had accepted, for the most part, the fact that she would never have a child. She had come to realize there were other goals she could pursue, that she could be happy without a husband and a child. Single, successful women were very common today. Many women were even choosing not to have children at all.

But her resolve had disappeared almost as soon as she met Jake Hunter, dear Jake who filled her life, who made her heart sing and laugh, who constantly reminded her she was a woman—a woman to be loved.

"You're right, Mother," Madeline said. "But being blessed does not always mean being happy."

Celia frowned. "And what do you think would make you happy, Madeline?"

Jake! Jake Hunter would make me happy, she wanted to cry to her mother. The problem was, could she make Jake happy? She shrugged indifferently. "I don't know for sure. I think it's going to take some time to know the answer to that."

The next afternoon Madeline had just come back from a walk on Front Street when the telephone rang. She snatched it up quickly, hoping desperately that it might be Jake. "Hello."

"Hello, Madeline. How are you? Did I catch you at a busy time?"

Madeline's heart sank at the sound of Maria's voice.

"No, of course not. How nice of you to call."

"I thought if you weren't busy you might come over to the shop. I've just gotten in a new shipment of dresses you might like to look over."

"Sounds lovely," Madeline agreed, glad for anything to occupy her time. "I'll be right over."

She changed from her sweaty shorts and jogging shoes to a soft pink shirtwaist and white flats, and then brushed her hair.

The drive over in Jake's Cadillac with the top down was warm, and she was grateful for the air conditioning when she entered Maria's boutique.

She noticed several customers browsing through the clothing and Maria, who was busy filling an empty clothes rack. As the bell over the door tinkled she looked up to see Madeline, waved and motioned for the younger woman to join her.

"I'm so glad you came," Maria said. "These things were just so delightful I thought you might want to take a look."

Madeline began studying the things Maria had already hung on the rack. There were florals of deep purple and bright turquoise and many things in yellow and black—colors that seemed to be everywhere in women's fashions these days.

"These are marvelous. Real trendsetters," Madeline exclaimed as she held a pleated skirt and matching jacket out in front of her. "Maria, you should have no problem selling these things."

"That's what I thought," Maria agreed. "That's why I called you over here. I know you're going to be my competition, but I can't help that. You're still like my own daughter so I had to share this with you."

"What?" Madeline asked curiously. She hung the jacket and skirt back on the rack and reached for a plaid dress with an enormous gathered skirt.

"I found these wonderful things at a buyers' show in Dallas. They're inexpensive yet very up-to-date. I think everyone from teenagers on up to middle-aged women will go for them."

"Yes, I do, too," Madeline agreed while wondering what Maria was getting at.

"They're having another show the first of next week. I'd love for you to go with me. How 'bout it?"

A trip to Dallas with Maria. Any other time she would have jumped at the opportunity. "I don't think—"

Maria's face clouded with disappointment. "You can't say no. There will be all kinds of fall things there. Just what you need to start off with."

Madeline smiled regretfully. "I know. But I don't even have a store yet. It won't be vacated for a few more weeks."

"Well, you could store the things in your mother's house or garage. She has plenty of room. Oh, come on, Madeline," she pleaded. "It will be such fun to have you with me. Fashions don't interest my husband. He always stays home, and I end up having to make these trips by myself. We'll stay a couple of days and do the town. It'll be great."

A part of Madeline wanted to say yes. She knew she would enjoy Maria's company and the chance to preview the fall fashions. But there was Jake and her promise to him: whatever he decided—one way or the other—she would be here when he returned. The first of next week was still several days away. There was a possibility Jake might finish the script and head on back to Natchitoches. She had to be here when he returned. It meant more to her than the fashions or her dress shop; it meant everything to her.

"I'm sorry, Maria. I just can't leave the city now. It's a bad time for me. Maybe we can plan something later on."

Maria smiled with understanding. "Of course we can. I'll hold you to it." She studied Madeline closely as she pulled another piece of clothing from the rack. "So may I take a guess? That handsome writer is keeping you here?"

Madeline looked at Maria disbelievingly. "Why do you say that?"

Maria's laughter could be heard throughout the boutique. "Madeline, I'm not that old! When he walked in here it was like dynamite going off. You looked at each other so—so intimately."

Madeline couldn't believe it. That had been only the day after she had met Jake! "We did?" she asked crazily.

Maria smiled. "Yes. You did. And I thought, Madeline knows what she's doing this time. This man will make her happy."

A soft red blush spread across Madeline's face. "Oh, Maria," she scolded. "You couldn't have known anything of the sort."

Maria laughed coyly. "Madeline, I do not have a little French blood in me for nothing. I know about love."

Madeline smiled, but she thought Maria may know about love, but she did not know of Madeline's problems. If she did, she might not be quite so ready to predict happiness for Jake and her.

For another hour or so Madeline explored Maria's boutique while the older woman discussed some of the problems Madeline might face with her own shop.

Madeline left the boutique feeling much more knowledgeable about the clothing business, but not the least bit happier. All she could think about was the fact that Jake was gone.

Sliding her sunglasses onto her nose, she turned the key in the Cadillac, then pulled out of the parking area. On impulse she headed south toward Highway 1. It was a beautiful, sunny day. She would just drive along and try to enjoy the scenery.

She took the same route she and Jake had taken the day of the rain storm, although it seemed very different for her now. Jake was not by her side laughing and teasing and making a nuisance of himself by trying to pull the hem of her dress up well over her crossed knees.

She had rapped his roaming hand a good one then. But later, when they had been soaked with rain, his hands had slid up her thighs and she had gloried in his touch. It had taken all her willpower to push him away.

At the folk museum she turned around and headed back toward Natchitoches. She barely let herself glance at the spot where she and Jake had sat in the car in the rain. The sight was just too painful.

She drove the Cadillac quickly on the way home. The sun was sinking lower in the sky and the air was cooling somewhat. The wind whipped her red hair out behind her, but it failed to dry the tears hidden behind the smoky lenses of her glasses.

Celia ran out on the front porch when Madeline pulled the long white car into the driveway. She was out on the concrete driveway by the time Madeline had a chance to pull the keys from the ignition.

"Maddie, where have you been? I've been worried out of my mind!"

Madeline looked at her mother, dazed. "Why?"

"Why?" Celia demanded. "You were gone! You didn't leave a note! I was afraid you'd broken down somewhere or had an accident."

"I'm sorry," Madeline apologized as she got out of the car. "I went over to Maria's boutique."

Celia frowned as her daughter shut the car door. "Maddie, darling. Maria's has been closed for nearly two hours. It's going on seven o'clock!"

Madeline glanced around her. She had been so caught up in her thoughts she hadn't realized it was getting late. "I'm sorry," she said once again. "I went driving around. I guess the time got away from me."

"Madeline, are you sure you're okay?" her mother asked as they both started toward the house.

"Yes, I'm fine," Madeline quickly assured her.

"Well, I fixed tacos for supper. There are plenty left. You can heat them in the microwave."

Madeline shook her head and started toward the staircase. "I'm not hungry, Mom. I'll just eat some melon or something later on."

Upstairs Madeline took off her sunglasses and washed her face with cold water. By the time she powdered her face, the tear stains were practically gone.

She was just about to leave her bedroom when there was a slight rap on the door. When she looked up, Celia was entering the room, a drink in each hand.

"Here." She handed Madeline one of the frothy cold drinks. "I made you a piña colada. So take a big drink of it and then tell me what it is that's got you so torn up."

Madeline glanced warily at her mother. "What makes you think I'm upset about anything?"

"Oh, come off it, Maddie," Celia admonished as she plopped down on Madeline's bed. "You've been acting strange for the last two days, ever since Jake left, to be exact."

Madeline took a sip of her drink, then swiveled around on the vanity bench so that she was facing her mother.

"I miss him," she said simply.

"Of course you miss him; so do I," Celia said. "But you don't fall to pieces just because you miss someone."

Madeline sighed. "Okay—I miss him desperately."

"Why?"

Madeline grimaced at her mother's persistence. "Oh Mother, do we have to go into this?"

"I think we'd better," Celia answered, running a hand through her short blond hair. "Because I know you, darling. You've always been one to keep your problems and feelings inside you. You bottle them up until they go round and round in that head of yours and become bigger than you can handle."

Madeline clutched the cold glass, knowing there was a lot of truth to her mother's statement. She did keep things in

side her, but she suspected that came from being married to
a man who had never wanted to communicate with her.

"I love Jake. And he's asked me to marry him. In fact, he
wanted me to go with him to the Keys and get married
here."

Celia's expression didn't alter, and Madeline knew the
news hadn't surprised her mother at all. Especially since she
and Jake had been inseparable the last few weeks.

"I see," Celia said softly. "So, why didn't you?"

"Why didn't I?" Madeline gasped. "Mother, you, more
than anyone, should know the answer to that!"

Celia frowned, then took a swallow of her piña colada.
"You mean your inability to have children. Have you told
Jake about it?"

Madeline nodded and Celia asked, "And what did he
say?"

Madeline's fingers trembled as they brushed tiredly across
her forehead. "He said it disappointed him, but that it
wouldn't change his love for me."

"Well," Celia said, smiling brightly. "There's no problem then, is there?"

"Mother," Madeline snapped. "How can you know that?
How can I know that Jake wouldn't regret it later on? I'd be
robbing him of one of life's greatest gifts. I love him too
much for that. I don't want to hurt him."

"You'll be hurting him more if you don't marry him. He
loves you. He wants to spend his life with you. That's what
really matters."

Madeline rose to her feet and paced around the spacious
bedroom. "That's easy for you to say because you have me.
You can't imagine what it's like to look at the future and
know when you die you won't leave a part of you behind,
that you can never give a child, a legacy of love and life."

Celia frowned with impatience. "Madeline, I thought you had come to grips with the fact that you can't have a baby. I thought you were putting all that behind you."

"I had! I did!" Madeline exclaimed. "But now I don' have just my feelings to consider. Jake is involved now."

Celia put her glass down on the nightstand, crossed th floor and put her arms around her daughter. "What you don't realize, my baby, is that children make up only a par of being married to someone. Asa and I had you, but i didn't make our marriage last. We just didn't have tha special kind of love, that special kind of need for each othe to make it work. You think your marriage to Andrew faile because you couldn't have a child. You thought a chil would have made everything right for you, but it wouldn' have, darling. You realize that don't you?"

"Yes," Madeline mumbled. "But Jake—"

"Jake is a man who might be a lot of laughter on th outside but on the inside things run very deep. He's a ma who doesn't take life's values lightly. If he says he loves you if he says it doesn't matter to him about the children, the you can believe him."

"Do you really think so?" Madeline asked hopefully looking into her mother's gentle face.

Celia smiled encouragingly. "I know so. And what yo need to know is that you and Jake have enough love be tween you to make a marriage work with or without a child You don't have to have the extra dimension a child gives marriage, because you already have so much to give eac other."

Madeline's heart began to lift. Her mother's word sounded so logical and so right. She did love Jake tha much. She was sure of it, and Jake loved her. Maybe the did have that special kind of love.

"Oh Mom," she said hugging Celia close. "You've mad me feel so much better. And—and when Jake gets bac home, and if he still wants me, I'm going to say yes! I've got to, Mom. I love him more than life!"

"Of course you do," Celia agreed happily while patting her daughter's shoulder. "And this time it will be right for you, baby. I know this time it will be right."

The telephone rang, and Celia answered it at the bedside table.

Madeline saw her mother smile widely. "Just a moment," she said. "She's right here."

Celia handed her the phone and then discreetly left the room.

"Hello?" Madeline said.

"Maddie, darling, your voice sounds wonderful! So say something else, like how much you've missed me."

Tears of happiness sprang to her eyes. Laughter and sobs threatened to strangle her. "Jake! Oh, Jake, I've missed you terribly!"

"It's been hell here without you, Maddie. I can't put two good sentences together," he admitted.

Madeline's heart soared at his husky words. "When are you coming home?" she asked quickly. "I can't stand it up here much longer if you don't come home."

"That's why I'm calling," he said. "The producer wants me to stay on through to the end of the week as sort of a consultant."

"That long!" Madeline groaned. "That's so far away."

"I know. But I couldn't very well tell him no."

Music and laughter could be heard in the background, plus a lot of loud talking. It sounded as though he was among a rowdy group.

"Jake, where are you, for Pete's sake?"

"I'm in a nightclub," he said, his voice rising as a man shouted out something in the distance. "The crew are throwing a party tonight. But forget the noise, Maddie. I just want to hear you say you'll be on a plane down here to-morrow.''

"Tomorrow?" she repeated, her head suddenly swimming.

"I still want to marry you, darling. I've done nothing but think about you, about us, and it's like I said. I love you. Nothing can change that. Please say you'll come Maddie. I'm dying without you.''

"I'm not doing so well without you, either," she told him.

"Does that mean yes? You'll come?"

How could she refuse him when her heart was bursting with joy just at the sound of his voice? "Jake—I—"

"I'll call the airport in Natchitoches and arrange to charter you a flight. I'll be waiting for you at the Miami airport."

"Jake—are you sure?" she began doubtfully. "I—"

"I love you, Maddie. Get down here and let me prove to you just how much.''

She began to laugh then. "All right, darling, I'll come! I'll be looking for you at the airport tomorrow.''

"Until tomorrow then.''

"Goodbye, love.''

Before she hung up the receiver she thought she heard a loud war whoop, and the voice sounded surprisingly like Jake's.

Madeline ran excitedly to the door and did a bit of yelling herself. "Mom! Mom! Come up here and help me!''

Chapter Nine

As the little airplane carried Madeline closer to Miami, she became more and more excited. She was going to meet Jake. They were going to be married!

Madeline smiled to herself as she recalled how ecstatic Celia had been to hear the news. She had hurriedly helped Madeline to decide which clothes to take and to pack them into suitcases.

At the airport her mother had given her at least a dozen last-minute instructions, and then said, "Tell Jake I'll take good care of Mr. Miles, but I won't feed him salmon or tuna like Maddie does." Then, with tears of happiness in her eyes, she had kissed Madeline goodbye.

Madeline smiled gently as she stared out at the fluffy white clouds below. I'm going to be happy, Mother, she vowed. Now, after a long, long time, I'm really going to be happy.

"Better buckle up, miss," the pilot said to her. "We're heading toward the airport."

Nervously she fastened her safety belt, then reached for her handbag. She pulled out a compact and snapped it open. The reflection in the tiny mirror showed green eyes shining with excitement, and smiling lips colored a soft peach that matched the glow on her cheeks.

Running a hand over her smooth red hair, she shut the compact and dropped it back into her handbag. She looked pretty. One glance at the pilot's face this morning when she had walked up to the plane had told her that much.

She was wearing a white straight skirt topped with a rust-colored cotton sweater that had a neckline so low in the front and back that she had been forced to go braless. But Madeline didn't care. She felt beautiful, sexy and in love. She was starting a new life with a wonderful man. She was leaving all her doubts and inhibitions in the past, where they belonged.

She got off the plane and tried to catch a glimpse of Jake among the throngs of tourists and business people who crowded the airport. Madeline stared around the busy terminal with despair. He hadn't told her exactly where to meet him. How was she ever going to find him?

Hefting up her two suitcases once again, she began to walk through a wide corridor, searching through the sea of strange people for Jake's handsome face.

He was nowhere to be seen, and after a few minutes she stopped and impatiently tapped the toe of her white shoe against the tile beneath her feet. Where was the man? she wondered, frustrated.

"Hey legs, how 'bout a kiss?"

Madeline squealed with pleasure at the sound of Jake's voice, and several heads turned in their direction. She whirled around to see him just as his hands reached for her waist. As he pulled her into his arms, she dropped the suitcases to the floor and flung her arms around his neck.

For long moments they forgot the people around them and kissed hungrily.

"You look gorgeous, Maddie!" he exclaimed when their lips finally parted.

"You look pretty good yourself," she said, and laughed.

Dressed in a light blue summer shirt and tan pleated trousers, he appeared even more deeply tanned than before. The gold watch on his wrist stood out in vivid contrast to his darkness. He was so handsome and vital-looking, so familiar and dear.

She raised herself on tiptoe and kissed his cheek once again. "I missed you, Jake."

He put one arm around her waist and reached for her bags with his other. "You don't know how much I missed my redhead! But now you're here. And you've made me one happy man!"

The airport was so huge it was a long walk to Jake's rented car. They finally found it at one end of an enormous parking area. He stowed away her cases in the trunk, then opened the door for her.

It was a dark blue sedan, shiny and new. As Jake joined her inside it he said, "It's nothing like the old Cadi, but I guess we can put up with it till we get back home."

Madeline laughed as she looked around the interior of the car. "I may get claustrophobia in this thing."

"Sorry, darling, they were all out of Cadillac convertibles."

They both burst into laughter and then Jake reached over and pulled her into his arms.

"Maddie, Maddie my love, do you know how happy you've made me?"

Tears stung her eyes and she clung to him tightly. "It couldn't be any happier than you're making me."

He suddenly put her away from him and reached over to unlock the glove compartment. "Let me show you what I've got," he said smugly.

Madeline watched him pull out some papers and a velvet jeweler's box.

"A marriage license," he said, holding up the papers. "And for you, my love," he announced, flipping open the blue box.

"Oh, Jake," she gasped. "I love it!"

The ring inside was a wide band set with three rows of small diamonds. It was uncanny how Jake seemed to know exactly what she would like.

"Here, let's see if it fits," he said, taking the ring from its velvet bed and placing it on Madeline's finger. "We only have an hour to get to the church."

"An hour!" Madeline gasped as she slipped the ring onto her finger. "We're getting married in an hour!"

He pushed and pulled at the ring to make sure it fit her while Madeline stared at him in amazement.

He grinned beguilingly at her, his gray eyes gleaming. "You didn't think we'd spend your first night here in separate beds, did you?"

"You lusty idiot," she murmured, feeling nothing but love for him. "You always want to do everything at a run."

"Not everything, Maddie," he corrected and planted a kiss on her lips.

"So where are we going to get married?" she asked, as Jake drove away from the airport.

"At a little church here in the city. Believe me, I've worked hard this morning getting all this arranged. Don't you think I deserve a kiss for it?"

Madeline chuckled and kissed him on the cheek. "Poor Jake," she said.

He glanced away from the traffic just long enough to brush his lips against hers. "I'll say poor Jake. When you become Mrs. Madeline Hunter I'll get a real kiss out of you!"

Madeline sighed and smiled contentedly. "Madeline Hunter. Sounds movie-starrish, doesn't it?" she mused dreamily.

He laughed and lifted his hand from the back of the seat to play with her red hair. "You can be Madeline Howard, too, if you want."

She cast him an intrigued look. "I guess I will be Mrs. Howard, too, won't I? But I think I like Jake Hunter, the real thing."

He grinned with amusement. "If Jake Hunter is the real thing, who is Harlon Howard?"

"Oh," she sighed melodramatically. "He's a rich, famous author who writes steamy novels, then tries to live up to them."

Jake bellowed with laughter. "Tonight I'll show you just where Harlon Howard leaves off and Jake Hunter begins!"

The church was a small white stucco structure with an arched doorway and palm trees lining the walk leading to it. Bright flowers grew in abundance around the front steps.

As Jake pulled to a stop in front of the church and shut off the motor, his expression grew serious. He sighed. "Madeline, I've just now realized that this is your wedding, too. You may have wanted something altogether different, a long fancy dress, a church full of family and friends. I—"

She hurriedly shook her head and placed her fingertips over his lips. "Jake, I had that once. It wasn't real. Where we are—what we have on—it doesn't matter. What matters is what we feel."

He held her close to him. "I love you, Madeline. I love you with all my heart."

The smell of freshly cut grass was heavy in the air when
they climbed from the car. Before they started up the walk,
Jake reached into the back seat and pulled out a box. It was
filled with yellow roses, which he placed reverently in Madeline's arms.

"You look exactly as a bride should look," he said.

Madeline looked up at him and curled her free arm
around his. She felt exactly as a bride should feel, too, because right at this moment her heart was bursting with love
for him.

William Black, the producer, and his wife, Lucille, were
waiting for them inside the church. They were an odd-
looking pair. William was a very small man with a practically bald head and dark-rimmed glasses framing small eyes.
Lucille was several inches taller and outweighed her husband by a good thirty pounds. Her hair was bleached plat-
inum and fluffed around her face in short curls. She was
pretty in a flamboyant way and Madeline supposed that
even though they seemed to be opposites there must have
been something that attracted them to each other. They were
in their fifties now and had been married for almost thirty
years.

The ceremony was short but touching. Jake and Madeline didn't take their eyes off each other the whole time the
minister spoke.

William and Lucille were both beaming with pleasure as
Jake kissed Madeline tenderly and thoroughly after the
minister pronounced them man and wife. The film tycoon
pumped Jake's hand heartily and kissed Madeline's cheek.
Lucille hugged them both while dabbing at the tears in her
eyes.

"Lucille, you're supposed to be happy, not sobbing,"
William told his wife.

Lucille sniffed and smiled. "I am happy," she pointed out. "Jake and Madeline are so in love that it makes me cry."

"Well, let's sign the papers so we can let these two get out of here and start their honeymoon," William said good-naturedly.

"How are you getting back to the islands?" Jake asked William and Lucille later as they all left the church.

"Boat. I didn't want that long drive."

"Madeline, don't forget to put your roses in water," Lucille reminded her.

"I won't," Madeline assured her. "And I thank you and Mr. Black for standing up with us."

"Oh, my dear, it was a pleasure! We've known Jake for ages and I'm really looking forward to getting to know you."

A minute or two more of good wishes and then the Blacks departed in a waiting taxi. Jake and Madeline drove away from the little church in the rental car.

Heading south, Jake spoke of the Overseas Highway that would take them to Key West. Madeline had never been to Florida or the Keys and she looked out at the flat, sandy landscape and endless palm trees with eager excitement.

"I don't know whether to look out at the scenery or to look at you," she said with a little breathless laugh.

"At me, Maddie! At me!" he exclaimed and she turned to see him grinning at her.

"Yes, I think I do like watching my handsome husband," she mused and smiled.

"Good, because we have several hours of driving ahead of us and I want your eyes right here," he said smugly, his finger tapping his jaw.

She looked at him disbelievingly. "You're teasing!"

"Yes," he chuckled. "I'm teasing." He put his arm round her shoulders. "This is your first visit to Florida. I

want you to look at everything. You're going to have m
around to look at for a long time to come."

Madeline snuggled happily against him and prepare
herself for the long drive ahead. In no time at all the
seemed to be speeding along by an endless expanse of wa
ter. In some places the ocean appeared blue, in others green
They passed over wild marshes, swamps with black, twiste
roots and tangles of dark green undergrowth. It was wild
isolated and strangely beautiful.

Some of the smaller islands had towns built on then
which catered mainly to tourists' needs. It was nearin
nightfall when Jake stopped at one of these towns to find
restaurant. Madeline was grateful, for they had been trav
eling a long while and her legs were stiff.

The place they chose had airy rooms with ceiling fans and
was decorated with an abundance of tropical plants. Ma
deline looked around them with interest as a waitress le
them to a table.

When they were alone once again Jake took her hands i
his.

"What do you think about the Keys?" he asked.

Madeline smiled warmly. "They're exactly as you de
scribed them in *The Legacy*. I felt I had been to these is
lands when I read the book. Now I know the feeling wa
right."

"What a nice compliment, Maddie," he said, and gentl
squeezed her fingers. "I can't wait for you to see Key West
It's such a contradiction: the city and the old town. I thin
you'll get a kick out of it."

Madeline laughed sexily. "I think I'd get a kick out o
anyplace as long as you're with me."

At that moment the waitress brought them steaming cup
of coffee. Jake took a drink of his before he said, "We'r
going to have such fun, Maddie. We'll travel all over th
States, see everything we want to see."

"I can't wait." Madeline sighed, then looked at him seriously. "Jake, where are we going to call home?"

He seemed surprised by her question. "Why, Natchitoches, of course. That's where your home and your mother are. I don't want to separate you two. Besides, you're going to have your dress shop there."

"You mean you still want me to go ahead with that?" she asked.

"Of course I want you to go on with it. It's important to you. In fact, I think I'd be a good partner, don't you? By the time we get back home the lawyers will probably be out. We'll look it over, and I'll tell you how much money I'm willing to invest in the business."

He winked at her, and Madeline's fingers tightened over his. She loved him so much; she loved him because he was kind and warm and understanding and simply because he was Jake.

"But how are you going to do that and have time for your novel?"

"Don't worry about the novel: it will get written. We'll share our time and interests together. However, I do think the first thing we should do is try to find a house. Does Celia know any good realtors?"

Madeline laughed, and her eyes danced with excitement. "Mother knows nearly everyone. She'll find us the perfect realtor."

"Good. I'll call my lawyer tomorrow and tell him to put my place in Atlanta up for sale. But as for the apartment in New York, I think we'll keep it. We might want to hop up here from time to time to take in some Broadway plays or just slouch around the city. What do you think?"

She shook her head incredulously. "I think you're running way ahead of me, Jake. Just when did you have time for all this planning?"

He laughed and ran a hand through his dark hair. "From the time I passed you on my motorcycle on Second Street and you turned up that beautiful little nose at me."

"Oh, Jake," she scolded. "You didn't even know me and I—"

Madeline's voice broke off as the gray-haired, middle-aged waitress arrived with their steak dinners. She placed them carefully on the table and turned to go, but Jake called her back.

"Was there something else you needed?" she asked.

"Yes," Jake said. "I want you to tell me something. Don't you think this is one of the prettiest women you've ever seen?"

Madeline blushed furiously. "Jake!" she scolded.

The waitress nodded and smiled warmly. "Very pretty indeed," she agreed.

Jake beamed with pride. "Well, this pretty lady married me today. Now don't you think that makes me about the luckiest man on earth?"

The woman laughed. "I'd say you're a happy man. Congratulations," she told them.

Madeline had just taken the last bite of her steak when the waitress returned to their table. She refilled their coffee cups and then surprised them both by bringing out a plate with a huge piece of cake on it. In the middle was a small lighted candle.

"Oh, how nice," Madeline murmured.

The overhead fan made the little flame flicker as the waitress placed the cake in the middle of their table.

"Sorry we didn't have something more traditional," she said, looking at the coconut confection. "But we hope you'll enjoy it just the same."

"Thank you," Jake told her. "It was very kind of you."

The woman smiled and left the room. Madeline glanced from the little candle up to Jake's dark, lean face.

"Shall we blow it out together?" she suggested.

Jake's gray eyes reflected the warmth of the candlelight as he looked at Madeline. "Yes. Together," he murmured.

They leaned down, put their heads together and blew. Smoke wafted up into their faces and in the other room the waitress smiled to herself as she heard their happy laughter ring out.

Chapter Ten

Madeline discovered, as Jake had promised, that Key West was a contradiction. The modern city was similar to most cities in the United States, but as they traveled farther and Old Town emerged, the picture changed drastically.

"Some people call it Conch Town. But whatever—it's the real Key West, where it all began," Jake told her as they drove through a street lined with white clapboard houses and white picket fences.

If it hadn't been for the lush tropical growth filling the yards, you could almost mistake this place for a New England town, Madeline thought, although she noticed a few touches of the Bahamas and the South as she studied the houses. Nearly all of them had wide porches, shutters in the windows and a great deal of Victorian gingerbread.

"Why do most of the houses have widow's walks built on the rooftops?" she asked Jake.

"Shipwrecks," he answered. "They were built up there so someone in the family could keep a watch out for ships during storms. Salvaging the goods from those wrecks used to be a big business.''

"That seems rather sad,'' Madeline mused aloud, "to make a profit over someone else's misfortune.''

"Surviving was hard in those days,'' Jake said. "I guess they did it any way they could.''

Not knowing exactly where they were going, she scooted to the edge of the seat when Jake pulled to a stop in front of a huge, dark house. It was located at the end of a street and isolated from the other houses by a big fence and a dense growth of underbrush.

"Is this where we're staying?'' she asked eagerly.

He nodded. "It belongs to the Blacks, but they wanted to let us have it when they heard we were going to be married.''

"They shouldn't have made such a sacrifice,'' Madeline said.

"It was no trouble for the Blacks,'' Jake chuckled. "They've rented a suite of rooms at a hotel for the duration of the shooting.''

It was dark, so Madeline couldn't tell much about the place, although she could see enough to know that the house was built a few feet above the ground—to save it from the dampness, she supposed. There was a huge tree in the front yard that looked a bit like a breadfruit, but she couldn't identify most of the other vines and tropical bushes.

"Lord, I'm glad we're finally here,'' Jake exclaimed as he tossed their suitcases onto a braided rug in the center of the floor.

"So am I,'' Madeline agreed as she looked around the main living room. "Oh, look,'' she said with utter surprise, spying a bucket of ice with a bottle in it. "Someone's left something for us.''

Jake quickly crossed to the side table and picked up a small piece of paper. "Best wishes, the Blacks,'' he read,

then lifted the bottle out of its bed of ice. "Mmm, a goo
label."

"How nice of them to think of it," Madeline said.

"I'll say," Jake replied, and Madeline smiled provoca
tively as a gleam came into his eyes. "So what do you say w
get out of these clothes and toast each other?"

Madeline rushed toward the door before he had a chanc
to get hold of her. "I've got to do one thing first," she calle
back to him.

"Maddie!" he shouted after her.

She ran down the front steps and out to the car. Her ye
low roses were still on the back seat and she picked them u
lovingly and carried them to the house.

Jake, the suitcases and the champagne were gone whe
Madeline entered the house, so she went to the kitchen an
filled a large vase with water. She was placing the slightl
wilted roses in the water when Jake appeared and kissed th
curve of her exposed shoulder.

Smiling, she turned to see him holding two filled chan
pagne glasses. He had taken off his shirt and Madeline'
heart beat wildly as her palms slid up his chest.

"Where did you put the rest of it?" she asked huskily.

He grinned and the chuckle that passed his lips was de
ilish. "In the bedroom, where else?"

She took the glass from him with a sly look and a so
laugh. Jake slowly curved his arm around her waist an
touched his glass to hers.

"To our love and our life together," he said.

"Our love, our life," she whispered.

After they had drunk part of their champagne, Jake b
gan to guide her out of the kitchen and down a small hal
"Now tell me, Maddie darling, did you bring that beautifu
white gown with you?"

She knew exactly which one he meant: the one she had been wearing when he had seen her out on the balcony that first morning.

"No, I didn't."

"Maddie," he groaned with disappointment. "I've dreamed of seeing you in that gown again! It's all I've had on my mind for weeks!"

"You're exaggerating." She giggled and pulled away from him.

Five minutes later, she emerged from the bathroom in a pale yellow silk nightgown. White lace edged the plunging neckline and brushed her bare toes as she walked toward him. It was close-fitting and hugged her womanly curves. Jake whistled as he sat in the middle of the bed and eyed her with sheer pleasure.

"Darling, I've already forgotten you have a white gown," he said.

Madeline laughed and joined him on the bed. "Well, you did say I could wear yellow better than a canary," she told him. Her head was swimming as she looked into his handsome face, but the dizziness couldn't be blamed on the champagne. No, it was all Jake's doing. The idea that she was finally going to make love with him was almost too much for her to bear.

"You remember that, eh?" he asked, threading his fingers through her long, copper-colored hair.

She rubbed her lips softly and sensuously against his. "My mind has been like a tape recorder where you're concerned."

Jake didn't take the time to turn off the bedside lamp. His hands moved to her bare shoulders, and he twisted her down on her back with one sudden movement.

As the mattress yielded softly beneath her, Jake covered her lips with his. He could find no words to tell her of his overwhelming need.

"I love you, Maddie," he moaned. "Let me show you— let me show you how much—"

"Yes," Madeline answered as his lips left her mouth and traveled down the tender arch of her throat.

Nothing had changed, she thought. That familiar ache for him was filling her, the same ache that had tormented her that day in the rain. "Show me, Jake. I want you so!"

"My wife," he groaned exultantly. "My beautiful wife."

His fingers slipped beneath the lacy straps of her gown, then pulled them slowly down her arms. The yellow satin fell away and his mouth sought her breast. His teeth nipped, his tongue teased, until Madeline arched and moaned his name. Her hands trembled as they slid down his back.

He was so hard, so warm and wonderfully masculine. He was the beat of her heart, the very core of her life and she knew suddenly and swiftly that she had never known real love until this very moment. She had never known what physical desire and physical need were really like until Jake had touched her.

She wanted to tell him all this. She wanted him to know the depth of her feelings, but there was just too much to tell. It would take a lifetime.

"My God, Maddie, I want you! I've waited for you for so long!"

She opened her eyes to find he was looking down at her. His finger reached out and traced her upper lip. It quivered beneath his touch and Madeline lifted her hands to his hair and tugged his mouth down to hers.

Jake moaned and pulled away from her just long enough to remove his undershorts, then reached to pull the night-gown down over Madeline's hips.

Her whole body felt hot and shivery as his hand slipped over her curves. "I wanted to go slow for you, Maddie," he whispered hoarsely. "I wanted to—but I can't. I can't wait—"

"I don't want you to wait, my darling," she said in a breathy voice. "I don't want you to wait another second—"

With an anguished moan his hands slipped beneath her hips and lifted her against him. Madeline cried out with the sudden, splendid shock of their merging bodies. He was glorious and dazzling! He was finally and completely hers!

There was no gentle rhythm to their lovemaking. There was too much hunger, too much love for that. Madeline didn't want to be gentle with him and she didn't want him to be gentle with her. She surged and writhed beneath him, sank her teeth into his skin and let her body ask for all that he could give her.

At the end, Madeline was so overwhelmed with sensations that she clung to Jake and cried his name over and over. The room was whirling madly around her and she was sure if she let go of him she would be flung out into space. So she held on and waited for her mind to clear.

Long moments later Madeline finally became aware that her cheek was lying against his chest and his heart was drumming in her ear. So this was making love, she thought wonderingly. This was what it was really like.

She lifted her head and smiled at him. "Are you still sorry I didn't bring the white gown?"

He grinned back at her and combed his fingers through her tangled hair. Her face was flushed and damp with sweat.

He had always supposed she knew all the mysteries and pleasures of passion, but Jake now realized that Madeline had been a stranger to real passion until now. It had been obvious to him from her reactions, from the way she had cried out in startled ecstasy. She had not been prepared to lose herself so completely and it pleased him to know that he had given her that mindless joy. Everything about her pleased him!

"I thank God you didn't bring the white gown, or I'd probably be suffering from cardiac arrest right now."

Madeline giggled and moved farther up on his chest so that she could kiss him on the mouth.

His arms shifted and moved around her waist. The gardenia-like scent of her hair stirred his senses, and he realized he would never get enough of this woman.

"Jake—I—I finally know what it means to give my body and soul to a man," she whispered. "I didn't know—I didn't—"

"You don't have to tell me, Maddie love. I was right there with you. I know, and I'm glad it was me."

She studied his face, while her fingers smoothed the strong line of his jaw. "Yes—I'm glad it was you, too," she said contentedly.

He kissed her again, and she rolled away from him and rose from the bed.

Jake watched her with infinite pleasure as she went to the table where the glasses and champagne were sitting.

Her body was perfect, he thought. Her breasts were firm and round; her waist was slender, and her legs were exactly the way a woman's legs were meant to be.

Looking at her now, his body still warm from their lovemaking, it was hard to believe she could ever doubt herself as a woman. It was even more difficult for him to understand that because of some biological problem she felt she had nothing to offer him. She was rich and fertile with love, and she filled him with satisfaction. He hoped that eventually she would come to understand this.

"I think we need another toast, don't you?" she asked. "You didn't let me finish the last one."

"By all means," he agreed, smiling smugly.

She handed him the filled glasses, then went back to the table and picked up Jake's cigarettes.

"What are you doing?" he asked as he watched her pull out a cigarette and place it between her lips.

"I'm going to light you a cigarette," she told him. "Isn't that how they do it in all those old movies?"

"Maddie! You don't smoke. You'll—"

Ignoring his warning, she lit the cigarette and inhaled deeply. Almost instantly smoke streamed from her mouth, and she coughed and spluttered in outrage. "Lord, Jake!"

"Bring me that thing," Jake laughed. "You can practice being a movie star later on."

Madeline didn't object. Laughing, she handed him the burning tobacco and took the glass he offered her. She balanced it carefully while getting into bed next to him. Jake stuck the cigarette between his lips and put his free arm around her.

"What shall we drink to this time?" she asked. Her head was already bubbly with excitement. She didn't know if it could handle the champagne. But tonight was such a special occasion she didn't care.

His cheek rubbed contentedly against hers. "To you. To me. And may God let us be together a long, long time."

"Yes," she said wholeheartedly, and clinked her glass against his.

Madeline rested her head against his shoulder and sipped the bubbly white wine while Jake smoked his cigarette. She felt drowsy and happy and she groaned in protest when Jake finally slipped out of bed and pulled on his shorts.

"Where are you going?" she asked curiously.

Beyond their bed were two wide folding doors. Jake had pulled them open and was now walking out onto the porch. The sea air wafted in and she could hear its restless rolling in the distance.

"I want to check on something," he told him. He walked down the steps out of her view.

In just a matter of seconds he called to her. "Come here, Maddie."

"Just a minute." She pulled on the yellow nightgown and followed him down the steps.

The backyard was actually just a small distance from the ocean. Madeline could see the waves rolling gently upon the sand just a few yards away.

Jake was not looking at the ocean, though. He was staring at the sky, and he motioned for Maddie to join him.

A bright orange moon had risen in the east, and Madeline gasped at the splendor of it against the tropical night. Jake put his arm around her shoulders and said, "If you think that's beautiful, I can't wait to show you the sunsets down here. They're so glorious that it's a ritual for people to gather on the docks and the beaches in the evening just to watch the sun go down."

"I want you to show me everything," she said, and he turned and pulled her into his arms.

"You're not sorry you married me?" he asked.

"Sorry! I've got to be the happiest woman alive!" she exclaimed.

Her answer thrilled him, and he began to hum a recent pop tune and dance Madeline around on the sand. She laughed and the stars and moon spun in her eyes as he turned her around and around.

The next thing she knew Jake was pulling her toward the beach. Just before they reached the water they both collapsed upon the warm sand.

"What we need is food," Jake said as he sat cross-legged and sifted sand through his fingers.

"Food! After all that supper we ate!" Madeline exclaimed. Then she looked at him and smiled. "I wanted to bring your Goo Goo bars to you, but I didn't know about taking them through the airport."

His laughter was rich. "A woman after my own heart!"

Suddenly he climbed to his feet and started toward the house. "Stay where you are," he told her. "I'll be right back."

Madeline obeyed, and while he was gone, she dug her toes into the sand and enjoyed the sea breeze on her face.

"I knew the Blacks would probably leave food in the cupboards," Jake said as he joined her on the sand once again.

He set a basket of fruit between them and Madeline suddenly decided she was hungry after all. She ate an apricot and a banana while Jake gorged on grapes and nectarines and told her all about conch shells.

After a while Madeline walked to the ocean's edge to rinse the sweet stickiness from her fingers. The water was warm like the wind, and she ventured farther, letting it lap around her ankles.

"You're getting that beautiful gown wet," Jake warned from behind her.

She smiled at him in the moonlight. "I don't care. It feels good."

He got to his feet and began to run toward her. "If that's the case, why not wet the whole thing?"

Realizing his intentions, Madeline tried to make a dash for the dry sand but she was not nearly fast enough. Jake gathered her up and tossed her out into the water before she could even put up a good fight.

"Jake! What if a shark is out here!"

He laughed heartily. "Do you think a shark would risk running aground just for a bite of your leg? On second thought," he said, "he just might, knowing how good your legs look."

By now he was beside her and she retaliated by splashing water at him.

Madeline was panting for breath by the time they made it
back to shore. She lay down on the wet sand and gazed up
at the sky. She had never felt so free, so loved, so blessed.

Jake appeared above her, obscuring the orange moon,
and she welcomed his lips upon hers. His tongue plundered
her mouth until she wound her arms around his neck and
urged him even closer. It was hard for her to believe that she
already wanted him again, yet she did. Little shafts of desire lanced through her. She nibbled at his small nipples and
the hair-roughened skin on his flat stomach.

"You're delicious when you're wet, did you know that?"
she asked.

He said nothing, simply pushing up the hem of her wet
gown to expose her soft thighs.

Madeline wound her legs around his as he covered her
with his weight. She could feel his desire against her and she
lifted her hips in a silent, wanton plea.

"We're outside. The neighbors," she reminded him huskily as he suckled her nipple through the wet satin.

"We have no neighbors," he murmured absently. "And
if we did they'd just think it was William and Lucille down
here."

The idea of William and Lucille wet and rolling around
in the sand made Madeline giggle furiously until Jake's
mouth finally found hers in the darkness.

After that Madeline gave herself up to loving her husband.

Chapter Eleven

The Legacy was going to make an exceptional movie. Madeline was certain of it. She was very proud of her husband's talents, and William Black was sparing no expense in producing the film.

Today they shot a scene that took place on the wharves. There were lots of stuntmen involved, guns exploding and a police helicopter whirring above their heads. It was all very exciting, even though it took a long time to shoot.

This was to be the final scene of the movie and it was a very complicated one. The stunt sequences had to go off just right or they would ruin the whole effect. When it was finally over the director fell, limp with exhaustion, into a chair. Poor William's balding head was a shiny, apple-red.

Madeline was relieved to see the scene finished. Now she and Jake could get on with their honeymoon. And since Madeline had fallen in love with the Keys, they were going to stay on a few more days before heading back to Louisiana.

To celebrate the final shooting of the movie, the cast and crew were all having dinner together downtown. Naturally Jake and Madeline had been invited and she dressed carefully before they drove back into the commercial part of the city for the party.

"Do I look all right?" Madeline asked for probably the tenth time as she and Jake neared the restaurant. She was wearing a pantsuit that showed off her long legs and draped softly over her full breasts. Andrew would never have allowed her to wear such things, and she supposed those old ingrained habits and doubts were hard to put aside. However, she was learning that Jake loved her to wear vivid, glamorous clothes, and he was constantly telling her how beautiful she looked.

He smiled indulgently and glanced away from the traffic to look at her. She was wearing a deep shade of forest-green and he thought he had never seen a woman so vibrantly beautiful. "You're going to make Paulette very jealous. She's accustomed to being the center of attention."

Paulette Dressler was the leading lady in the film. She was a petite brunette with limpid blue eyes. Madeline could hardly see why she would be jealous of anyone.

"Paulette was very good, what I saw of her," Madeline said. "Are you satisfied about the script as a whole?"

He nodded. "Yes, but I'm really just glad the film is finally finished. It's been hell having to sit around that set for the last two days instead of spending time with you."

Madeline was inclined to agree with him. "Well, just think of it this way: William was paying you a hefty sum just to sit there in case you were needed, not to mention the rest of the money you'll make on the film."

They pulled up at the restaurant. Jake handed the keys to the parking-lot attendant and began to guide Madeline toward the building.

"Being with you is worth more than any money I could ever make," he said to her, making Madeline's heart leap with love.

The night was very warm but the air conditioning made it cool and pleasant inside the huge restaurant. In one section there were three long banquet tables reserved for their party. Many of the guests had already arrived.

Madeline spotted Lucille and William immediately, and the older woman waved eagerly to them. "Over here, Maddie. You and Jake can sit with Bill and me."

"Nothing like being a celebrity. Doesn't it feel good?" Jake whispered wickedly in Madeline's ear as they quickly approached the Blacks.

She discreetly nudged him in the ribs and smiled warmly at Lucille. "How nice to see you again," she said, sitting next to the woman.

Jake refused to be separated from Madeline so William got up from Lucille's side and moved down to the other side of Jake. Madeline was embarrassed by the whole thing but Jake merely put his arm around her and smiled at her flushed face.

"William doesn't mind changing seats. He remembers how it was to be a newlywed, don't you?" Jake asked the wiry, little producer.

William lifted his cocktail glass and winked at Lucille. "I sure do, boy. Seems like yesterday."

Madeline smiled, thinking how wonderful it was for William to still be so infatuated with his wife after all these years.

Lucille blushed. "Bill, that was years ago," she protested.

"Beautiful years, Lucy," William said, sipping at his cocktail. "Beautiful years."

Madeline suddenly remembered the night she and Jake made love on the beach. She also remembered Jake's com-

ment that the neighbors would think it was the Blacks. She
loved this dear couple, but that did not prevent giggles from
bubbling up in her throat, and she frantically tried to swallow them.

The fact that she was in a public place with dignified
people all around her only served to make the matter worse.
As the others at the table began to look at her questioningly, she desperately took a deep breath and swallowed
once again. It helped. She was getting a grip on herself. That
is, until she saw the look in Jake's eyes.

He placed his hand over hers. "Madeline? Are you all
right?" he asked.

She smiled at him, and then thoughts of the beach popped
into her mind once again. A strange gurgling sound slipped
past her lips, then she began to cough in earnest.

"Madeline dear? Are you ill?" Lucille asked with much
concern.

Madeline shook her head and reached for a water glass.
"No, really I'm fine, Lucille. I—I think I picked up something on the beach the other night."

"Oh, you should be careful," Lucille insisted. "Sometimes the sudden change of climate can do strange things to
you."

Madeline swallowed several gulps of water and tried to
control herself. She chanced a glance at Jake, who simply
looked at her smugly. He knew everything that was running through her mind.

Lord, what a difference, she thought. If she had burst into
giggles in Andrew's presence he would have been furious. If
she giggled tonight she knew Jake would laugh right along
with her. It was a wonderful feeling.

"Are my bad, unconventional habits rubbing off on you,
darling?" he asked in her ear.

Beneath the table she pinched his leg and turned her attention to Lucille. "Your hair looks especially beautiful to

ight," she told the woman. "Did you try a different hairdresser?"

The night turned out to be a very enjoyable one. Madeline remembered many of the faces from her visits on the set. Everyone was very friendly.

Shrimp was served with a host of accompanying side dishes, and Key lime pie was the dessert. Madeline was stuffed but she ate every bite of the delicious pie.

Paulette Dressler was at their table, glittering in diamonds and a blue silk dress. She listened attentively as Jake and William discussed Jake's new novel.

Madeline supposed Paulette wanted a chance at a role in it, too, should it be made into a film. The idea was incredible to Madeline. The novel about Louisiana was just now at its very beginning, yet William and Paulette were discussing it as though a movie from it would be a smash.

"Whoa," Jake finally told them. "I've hardly begun the novel. It will be months before I get it anywhere near completion."

"Well, I just hope you've got a fiery, dark-haired vixen in it, darlin'," Paulette said in a mock southern drawl. "I've always wanted to play a vixen."

Jake exchanged knowing looks with Madeline while David Warren, the male star in *The Legacy*, spoke up from the opposite side of the table.

"That's enough about the novel. I for one want to know how Jake found such a beauty to marry him."

Jake laughed and squeezed Madeline's fingers. "That's easy, David. I picked her up on the street."

"Jake!" Madeline exclaimed.

Lucille and Paulette looked properly shocked, but the men merely laughed.

"Well, it's true, darling," Jake went on with obvious pleasure. "There's no use trying to hide it."

"Jake, stop lying and tell them how it really was," Madeline demanded.

"Yeah, Jake. Stop lying," one of the crew members said. "We know you don't pick ladies like Madeline up off the street."

Several more seconded that notion. Finally Jake shook his head and placed his hand solemnly over his heart. Madeline groaned when she saw the gesture.

"I swear guys. I did pick her up," Jake insisted. "Although, I will admit, she was a bit difficult at first."

The male crew members looked at him as though they knew they had a good storyteller among them and they couldn't wait to hear every line.

"I came speeding past her on my Harley-Davidson when I suddenly realized she needed a man's assistance. I slammed on the brakes, came back and offered her a ride on my bike. But," he drawled with mock regret, "she gave me the cold shoulder."

"What did you do?" David asked.

"What any red-blooded man in my situation would have done. I knew I had to impress her some way. I took the Harley home, got my Cadillac, drove it back to where she was and told her to load up."

"Oh, man, Jake!" one of the cameramen groaned. "I don't believe a word of this!"

Madeline smiled smugly and folded her hands in front of her. "Okay, Jake, now tell them how my mother just happened to be your landlady and that since you lived in my backyard there was really no way I could get away from you."

"Yeah!" one of the men shouted. "Now that sounds more like it!"

Jake smiled a bit sheepishly, then turned to Madeline and kissed her soundly on the lips.

"And I'm so glad you couldn't get away," he said to her

The next five days were glorious ones for Madeline and Jake. They swam, ate and slept whenever they wanted. He knew the Keys as well as any native, and he showed her things she would remember the rest of her life.

They explored many of the tourist shops and Jake bought her several pieces of clothing and jewelry. Madeline had never known anyone as generous as Jake. He constantly wanted to buy things for her. Naturally, he had plenty of money to do it, but something told her that Jake would do exactly the same thing even if he were penniless. His generosity didn't come from his bank balance; it came from his heart.

During their last day in the Keys, Jake chartered a boat and it sailed them all around the islands. They lay on the deck and soaked up the sun and even tried their hands at saltwater fishing. It was a beautiful trip, and Madeline told Jake she must have gotten some of her father's sailing blood in her veins. She had been captivated by the sun, wind and water ever since she had arrived in the Keys. Jake promised to bring her back on their six-month anniversary.

The airport in Miami was crowded when she and Jake boarded a jet to start their journey back home.

As they settled in their seats, Jake asked, "Are you sorry to be leaving Key West?"

Madeline looked away from the window to her husband. She shook her head and smiled. "No, not really. I loved it there, but it will be nice to get back to Natchitoches and start our new life together."

He clasped her hands in his. "Yes, it will be fun," he agreed. "I just hope Mr. Miles forgives me for deserting him."

Madeline chuckled. "We'll just give him a can of Mother's salmon; that will win him back over."

Jake laughed along with her; however, a moment later his expression grew serious. "You're sure you don't mind

stopping to see my dad and sister in Atlanta before we g
home? We could put it off to a later time.''

"Of course I don't mind,'' she told him. "It would b
mean of us not to see them. You called to let them know w
were married. They're bound to be curious about me.''

Jake grinned. ''Dad will be more than curious when h
sees you. He's like me; he's always had an eye for beautifu
women. It's a weakness in us Hunter men, I suppose.''

He began stroking her calf with his finger. Madelin
brushed it away and smiled wryly. ''Well, I hope he ha
better control over himself than you do,'' she told him.

Jake's devilish laughter elicited a frown of distaste fror
an elderly couple sitting across the aisle from them. Bu
whenever Jake's hand came back to rest upon Madeline'
knee she was sure she caught a hint of envy on the woman'
face.

Madeline couldn't believe her eyes when their taxi pulle
to a stop in front of Jake's house.

"You want to sell this?'' she asked in dismay.

It was a beautiful split-level home with at least a two-acr
yard. There was a four-car garage and a huge swimmin
pool, plus a beautiful white gazebo.

"Why not?'' he asked. "It's just a house.''

After their cases were unloaded he paid and tipped th
driver. Madeline helped him carry the suitcases up to th
front entrance.

"Madeline, I've been much happier in your mother's ol
cabin than I ever was here,'' he assured her.

Madeline was happy to hear this, but she hated to thin
he was selling his home because of her.

"Maybe so,'' she said doubtfully. "But this is reall
grand.''

He unlocked the door, leaned over and kissed her. "We'll find a really grand place in Natchitoches. And if we're lucky maybe it'll be right on the river."

Nothing seemed to pose a problem for him, Madeline thought. She hoped that after a while his attitude about things would rub off on her.

"Actually, I never would have bought this house if it hadn't been for Mother. She thought I should have something befitting a successful writer." He smiled at the memory. "She was very proud of me."

"I'm very proud of you, too," Madeline said with a cocky little smile.

Chuckling, he lifted the telephone and began to dial his sister, Loretta. As he talked with her, Madeline wandered through the opulent house. Her mother's home was beautiful, but this place was incredible. She wondered if Jake had entertained here very much and whether he had live-in help. Someone had to be doing the upkeep.

Madeline was exploring the game room when she heard the faint sound of a doorbell. Curious, she returned to the main living area. A tall man with a muscular build and dark hair had his arm around Jake's shoulder and was laughing heartily. She couldn't see his face, but when she stepped down into the room he looked up and spotted her.

It was as if she were seeing an older version of Jake. The man had the same coffee-colored hair, but his was threaded with silver. He also had the same gray eyes and the same grin.

"Hello," he said, offering her his hand and smiling broadly. "I'm Jake's dad, Howard Hunter."

Madeline placed her hand in his. Instead of shaking it he kissed the back of it, making her blush slightly. He was just like Jake!

"It's nice to finally meet you, Mr. Hunter."

"Call me Howard, darlin'," he insisted, then gave his son a sly smile. "I can see why you haven't been around lately with a new wife like this. I'm surprised you're giving us even one day."

"Can you blame me?" Jake countered, making his dad laugh again.

"Not a bit," he told his son, then said to Madeline, "You're a very lovely young lady. Welcome to the family. You don't know how happy it makes us to know that Jake has finally found himself someone."

"Thank you," Madeline murmured sincerely.

"How did you know we were here?" Jake asked his father.

"Loretta said you were flying in today. I took a chance and drove by on my lunch hour."

"Would you like a drink or something?" Madeline asked. "If I know Jake, he's surely got something around here."

Howard laughed and shook his head. "No, thank you, Madeline. I've just stopped by for a minute. I've got to be at a meeting in less than half an hour."

"Listen to the old man still running here and there trying to make a buck," Jake teased.

"There are some people in the world who have to work Jake. We can't all be like you," Howard said dryly.

Jake groaned good-naturedly and said, "I was just on the phone with Loretta. She's fixing supper for us. Are you going to be able to make it?"

"Wouldn't miss it," he said, already moving to the door.

After Howard had left, Madeline shook her head. "It' amazing," she said. "You look as if you were stamped righ out of the same mold."

"Thank you, sweetheart. I happen to think my father' pretty great."

"He seems wonderful," she said walking to the ivory-colored velvet sofa and reclining against the bright throw pillows in one corner.

Jake watched her every move. She looked so sexy in her cream-colored slacks and mint-green blouse. He couldn't believe the constant physical desire he had for her. He was addicted to her, and he had a feeling the great Louisiana novel was going to be some time in the making.

He crossed the room and knelt beside her. Madeline reached out and touched his face. The corners of her soft lips tilted sensuously. She couldn't believe how much she wanted and needed this man. They had made love endlessly down in the Keys, yet the urge to do so again and again was still with her. Every time she looked at him she wanted to be in his arms.

"We have a few hours before we have to be at Loretta's," he said huskily.

She looked at him innocently as her fingers played with the lapel of his white shirt. "Mmm, a few hours," she repeated languidly. "What shall we do? Get some of your things ready to ship to Louisiana?"

"Hardly," he drawled. He reached up and began to slip the pins out of her French twist.

"If I didn't know better I'd think you're insatiable," she whispered, but already her fingers were making short work of the buttons on his shirt.

The next moment Jake pulled her from the couch and down onto the soft carpet. "Let me show you just how insatiable," he said before his mouth covered hers.

Chapter Twelve

Jake's sister, Loretta, lived only a few minutes away. Her house was not nearly as spectacular as Jake's. It was a two-story, homey affair with white siding and black shutters. Grease stains marked the driveway, and Jake had to swerve to miss two bikes and a tricycle.

The yard was surrounded by a chain-link fence. Out on the grass were one of those red wagons that children can't seem to do without and a yellow dump truck filled with sand.

As Jake shut off the motor, Madeline felt something tighten and freeze inside her. She wanted to meet Jake's family and to become a part of them, because she loved him so much. But she wasn't sure she was ready for this—the children, the reminders. However, they were here and she couldn't disappoint Jake. She hoped she'd never disappoint him.

They were just starting up the walk when a woman in blue jeans and a blue tank top appeared on the front steps. She was tall and slim, younger than Jake but older than Madeline. Her hair was toffee-brown and was pulled back into a curly ponytail.

"Jake," she squealed, rushing down the steps.

She hugged him with great enthusiasm, then turned to Madeline. "Oh, you lucky, lucky old dog," she told Jake. "How did you ever manage to catch her?"

Madeline laughed. "Don't ask. You'll never hear the truth from him."

Loretta hugged Madeline with sisterly affection. "Welcome to the Hunter family, Madeline."

Loretta grabbed her by the hand and began to pull her toward the house. "Come on, I was just about ready to put the steaks on the grill," she told them.

"Where are Tom and the kids?" Jake asked as they entered the quiet house.

"Unfortunately, Tom was called out to the trucking yard. Some kind of loading problem or something," she explained. "But the kids are out back and the boys are dying to see you."

As they walked through the house Madeline looked wistfully around her. Toys were scattered here and there. On one end of the couch, bright red yarn hung in a tangled mass from what looked to be the beginning of a sweater. The kitchen was warmer than the rest of the house and smelled of spicy barbecue, making it obvious Loretta had been busy cooking.

It was the kind of home Madeline had always wanted. A place where there was love and chaos, children's laughter and tears. She tightened her hold on Jake's hand and tried not to think about it.

She noticed the backyard was enclosed with chain-link fencing also. Two oaks shaded a portion of it and the house. It was under the trees that Loretta had the barbecue going.

Madeline didn't have much time to notice anything else because as soon as they stepped out onto the concrete patio, three boys ran to Jake, tackling him around the knees.

Jake laughed and tussled with each of them while Loretta yelled, "Boys, please quiet down and show Madeline that you're not really heathens."

They calmed down enough to study Madeline with an intensity that belied their years.

"Maddie, this is Tim," Jake said, introducing the smallest boy. He was blond, had blue eyes, and looked like a little cherub.

"It's Timothy, not Tim," the little boy corrected his uncle.

"Oh, yes, Timothy. I always forget, don't I?" Jake winked at Madeline. "Timothy is four. And this is Michael, who is seven."

Michael, who was missing one tooth, had light brown hair and eyes like his mother's. He grinned broadly at Madeline. "Uncle Jake is my uncle," he proudly informed her.

Madeline smiled back at him. "Yes, I know."

The last and oldest of the boys was blond also. His name was Joel and he was nearly eleven years old, Jake told her.

Joel gazed at Madeline with something like awe. "You sure are pretty," he said. "Are you a movie star?"

Jake laughed and Madeline shook her head.

"No, Joel. Not anything nearly that exciting, but thank you for the compliment."

Michael began to tug on Jake's jean leg. "Come play football with us, Uncle Jake," he begged. "Joel got a new one for his birthday!"

Joel and Timothy began to pull Jake backward while Loretta threw up her hands in despair.

"Boys, please give Jake a minute to catch his breath. Go get the football, then you can play catch among yourselves until Jake gets ready to play with you."

All three boys scrambled toward the back door of the house, shouting every inch of the way. Loretta let out a deep sigh when they disappeared from sight.

"I don't know if I'll survive that crew," she said, brushing the bangs from her forehead.

"They're handsome boys," Madeline said sincerely. "You must be very proud of them."

Loretta smiled. "Yes. It's not always easy raising four children, but in the end all the effort is worth it. They're the light of my life."

"I know what you mean now that I've found the light of my life," Jake said with a pointed look at Madeline.

Loretta went to the grill. "Sit down, Madeline. I'll just put these steaks on and then we'll relax. Jake, why don't you fix us some drinks?"

"In a minute," he said. "I want to see Elizabeth. Where is she?"

Loretta pointed toward a playpen standing in a shady corner of the patio. "Asleep—I think."

Jake headed to the playpen, and Madeline followed somewhat reluctantly. She wanted to see the baby, but she dreaded it, too.

The little girl was lying on her stomach, but as Madeline and Jake neared the playpen her little legs drew up under her, making her diapered bottom stick up in the air.

She was waking, making soft little baby noises, so Jake reached down and lifted her from the playpen. Madeline noticed he held her as easily as if he had been a father for years.

"Here's my girl," he crooned to the baby. "She knew it was time to wake up and see her Uncle Jake." He kissed her on both fat cheeks, then held her to the side so that her face was pressed against his.

"Look at this, Maddie," he beamed with pride. "Now can you believe how much this little doll looks like me?"

Incredibly, she did look like him. Her hair was dark, almost the exact shade of Jake's, and her blue eyes had a silvery shade to them, as if they might later turn gray. She even had the hint of a broad-bridged nose like his.

"Naturally Jake thinks she's going to be a Miss America," Loretta told Madeline.

"She is a beautiful baby," Madeline agreed in a small voice, but she felt like crying.

"Of course she's going to be gorgeous," Jake said with conviction. "Probably she'll be a brilliant author, too."

Loretta laughed but Madeline could barely summon enough joy inside her to smile. She just kept looking at Jake and the baby he was cradling so tenderly in his arms.

"Come on, Elizabeth," he said to the baby. "Let's get something to drink. Your mother is a pitiful hostess."

"Jake, the day I have to start playing hostess to you will be a cold day in you-know-where," Loretta teased her brother.

Jake laughed and carried Elizabeth with him to a redwood picnic table where several plastic jugs of drinks were sitting, along with a small chest of crushed ice. Madeline followed him to offer assistance.

"What do you want, darling?" he asked Madeline after Loretta informed them she'd like some iced tea.

She peeked underneath the lids of the jugs. There was tea, lemonade and fruit punch. "I'll take tea, too," she said.

After Madeline helped him fix the glasses she took the teas to Loretta, who was busy cooking steaks at the grill. Jake took Elizabeth and his glass of punch to a folding lawn chair on the patio.

"I hope you let her have this stuff," Jake told Loretta. He was letting the baby drink from his cup and the red fruit juice was dripping from her chin. Jake began to wipe it off with his fingers.

"It's fine," Loretta assured him. "She loves it."

"That's obvious," Jake said with amusement. Every time he let the little girl have a drink she kicked and waved her arms with glee.

Madeline stayed at the grill and watched Loretta turn the steaks. The sight of Jake and the baby was too painful for her. It was obvious he was enchanted with the child, and it filled Madeline with a great sense of guilt and loss. She hated the feeling, but still she couldn't shake it off.

The boys burst back out of the house with their football. Loretta sent them to one corner of the yard so that the adults wouldn't get whacked in the head by a stray kick or pass. They yelled at their uncle often so that he could watch their achievements.

After a while Madeline forced herself to join Jake and Elizabeth. She pulled up a lawn chair beside them and gave him the brightest smile she could muster. She couldn't let him see that her heart was breaking. Not for anything did she want to spoil this time with his family for him.

Elizabeth seemed to find Jake's gold watch the most interesting thing about him. Her fat little fingers tugged and pulled at it desperately, trying to pull it from his wrist.

To divert her attention he pulled a thin leather wallet out of his pocket and gave it to her. Naturally, she tried to put it in her mouth and Jake said, "Loretta, either you're starving this child, or she's already developed a taste for expensive things."

Loretta chuckled and left the steaks to take care of themselves. She pulled up a chair beside Madeline and took a long swallow of iced tea.

"She's teething, brother dear. She likes anything she can chew on." She motioned toward the wallet. "You'd better get that away from her. She'll ruin it."

Jake frowned at his sister. "Do you think I'd be so mean as to give it to her and then take it back? Not a chance. It's waterproof."

"But is it tooth proof?" Loretta asked.

Jake's dark brows arched with amazement, and he looked down at the baby girl in his lap. "Does my little darling have a tooth?" he asked.

He proceeded to run his finger over her gums. Elizabeth clamped down and Jake pulled his finger back with a sudden jerk and a loud "Ouch."

"You little imp," he told the baby, and retaliated by giving her a big bounce on his knee, which Elizabeth responded to with gurgly laughter.

Loretta shook her head hopelessly at Madeline. "Madeline, I guess you can see if you have any children Jake will have them spoiled rotten before they're ever born."

Madeline felt the color drain from her face. Her heart thudded erratically and her features felt frozen. She tried her best to smile back at Loretta and found the effort was actually painful. "Yes, I'm sure he would," she said, hoping her voice didn't sound as stiff to Loretta as it did to her own ears.

Jake was so busy bouncing Elizabeth on his lap he didn't hear his sister's comment. Madeline looked at the woman and for a minute she actually contemplated telling Loretta the truth about herself. But she couldn't.

She looked at Jake and wondered why she felt shaky and cold when the temperature had to be in the mid nineties.

Howard arrived just as Loretta and Jake were taking the steaks off the grill. Above everything else, Madeline noticed he was, like Jake, a happy man. He laughed often and teased the boys mercilessly.

As they ate the steaks, potato salad and baked beans, Howard and Loretta asked to hear all about their honeymoon and how the filming had gone.

When the conversation turned to Jake's career, Howard began telling Madeline just how his son came up with the pseudonym Harlon Howard.

"It was actually his mother's idea. When she found out just exactly what kind of book Jake was writing she was frantic."

"You would have had to know Mother to really appreciate this, Madeline," Loretta told her. "Mother was this little thing who wore a size five shoe and presented this sweet demure appearance to the public. But at home she'd chase Jake and me around with the broom if we disobeyed her."

Jake smiled at the memory and Howard went on. "Sadie couldn't imagine all her proper friends reading Jake's raunchy novel—that's what she called it—knowing it was her son who'd written it. She told Jake there was no way he could let the publishers use his real name. He could use a pseudonym and if any of her friends should ask her what Jake did for a living she wouldn't lie completely. She'd just tell them he wrote those nice, pretty travel brochures."

Madeline looked at her husband with a bit of amusement. "What did you say to that?"

He shrugged. "I said okay. I wouldn't have embarrassed Mother for anything. Besides, I didn't care whose name was on the cover. I just wanted it in print one way or another. But tell her the rest, Dad," he said.

Madeline looked down the table at Howard. He was chuckling now; so was Loretta.

"Well, Sadie decided that it was only fair to Jake to make the name a family name, but one that no one would recognize. She used her father's name Harlon and my name Howard. She thought it was catchy and no one would ever guess it was Jake. But the best part is when the book came out. It became a big hit, a bestseller for some time. Sadie couldn't stand it. Her son was a bestselling author and none of her friends knew it. So she got on the telephone, called all her friends and tried her best to convince them that Harlon Howard was really Jake. She decided the book wasn't quite that raunchy after all.''

"Poor Mom." Jake chuckled. "She wanted me to put my real name on the next book, but it was too late for that. The name Harlon Howard already had the public's attention. The publishers liked it and didn't want to change it.''

Later, as Madeline helped Loretta clean up the dishes, she thought about Howard's story of Jake's pseudonym. The whole thing made it obvious just how much a family man Jake really was. The entire evening had proved to her just how deeply he valued family ties.

She pushed the soapy rag over a dirty saucepan while she gazed out the window. Jake and Howard were playing football with the three boys. They were all laughing and having a good time. She wished she could feel as happy as they, but she couldn't. She kept thinking how it would be in the future, how it would be when they gathered for Christmas and other holidays. Jake would never have the joy of seeing his own children grow and mature. He'd never see them carry on his name as Jake had done for Howard.

She looked at Elizabeth and saw how perfect and precious she was, then she looked again at Jake and her heart twisted. When they made love it was so beautiful. Why did things have to be the way they were?

"Jake is enjoying himself with the kids," Loretta said as she dried the saucepan Madeline had just rinsed. "But then he's always loved children. He's got much more patience with them than Tom has, but I suppose that's because he's not with them every day."

Madeline wished Loretta would stop talking about Jake and the children. She didn't want to hear any of it.

"You know, Jake nearly married once. I guess he told you."

Madeline nodded. "Yes, he did."

"She was a model from New York City. Jake met her while he lived there. Colette was pretty, but kind of offbeat if you know what I mean. Not at all like Jake. He wanted children, but she refused to have any. I think that's what finally opened his eyes to her because he left her shortly after that." Loretta looked warmly at Madeline. "But you're just perfect for him, Madeline. I can already see that. I'm so happy you two got married."

Madeline made a suitable reply then asked Loretta if she would excuse her for a moment. Once out of Loretta's sight she rushed to the bathroom and locked the door behind her.

Her heart was pounding and her hands were slick with perspiration. Her thoughts returned to the day she had asked Jake if he'd ever been married. "I came close once, but we had totally different values," he had said. Suddenly she was in the cabin and she had just told Jake she couldn't bear children. "I'm disappointed," he had told her, "but it doesn't matter. It's all right."

Oh, Jake, she thought with stabbing despair, my darling Jake, why did you marry me?

Chapter Thirteen

The house was dark and terribly quiet. Jake's soft, rhythmical breathing was the only sound in the bedroom as Madeline lay next to him.

It had been hours since they had left Loretta's. They had come home and made love and Jake had eventually fallen asleep.

Madeline, however, had not drifted off to sleep. She lay in bed staring into the darkness. The man she loved was sleeping, strong and warm beside her, yet her mind and her emotions were in turmoil.

A part of her wanted to forget everything—forget the joy Jake had expressed over Loretta's children, forget the fact that he had left one woman because she would not give him children. She wanted to pretend it had never happened and to go on taking the love and happiness he gave her.

But how could she? She was cheating him and deluding herself. She should never have given in to the impulsive desire to marry him. She had wanted him to think about the situation for a long time. She had wanted to think about it for a long time herself. Yet when he had left for Key West she had missed him terribly. She had wanted to believe that her inability to have a child would not matter to either one of them. Obviously, that had been the biggest delusion of all. Meeting Jake's family had proved it.

Jake's arm was folded possessively over her waist and gently she slid from beneath it. Quickly and silently she dressed in the darkness, then groped her way to the living room.

There was only one thing in her mind now and that was to get away. She needed time to think. She needed space so that she could step back and look at their marriage from a different perspective. If she tried to discuss it with Jake, she knew exactly what would happen. He would dismiss her doubts and try his best to convince her that all that mattered was their love for each other. And Madeline would still be left with that same helpless, guilty feeling she was experiencing now.

Without considering it any further, she dialed for a taxi. While she waited for it, she wrote a note to Jake and left it on his suitcases, which were ready and waiting for their departure the next day.

My darling, I have gone home without you. I hope you'll forgive me, but I had to have some time alone to think. Tonight when I saw you with Elizabeth and the boys I was suddenly reminded of all the things you would miss if I remain your wife. I love you so much that I can't bear to think of taking those things away from you, Jake. I want you to have everything you deserve—including children. I can't give you those children and it fills me with a great sense of guilt and sadness. Right now I just don't know if I can bear up under the weight of it. Madeline.

Since it was past eleven there was hardly anyone at the bus station. Madeline was grateful. She couldn't seem to stop crying no matter how hard she tried.

Images of their happy times in Key West tortured her. Everything had seemed so idyllic during their honeymoon. But that time in the Keys was a time set apart. Natchitoches wasn't a tropical paradise. They would have to deal with day-to-day reality there. Under those circumstances, how long would it be before he began to regret that all she had to give him was herself?

Somewhere in Mississippi she closed her red, puffy eyes and tried to sleep. The bus droned through the sultry summer night, carrying her closer to Natchitoches. But Madeline had a feeling that even Natchitoches wouldn't give her the answers or the security she needed this time.

It was mid-morning when Madeline got out of a cab in front of her mother's house. Jake's Cadillac and motorcycle were parked to one side of the drive. The sight of them tugged at her heart. She was a very different woman from the one he had picked up on Second Street. The trouble was, she wasn't quite different enough.

There was a note left on the fridge.

Dear Maddie and Jake,
    If you should happen to come home today, I've gone with Charles over to Toledo Bend Reservoir. Will be staying with friends till day after tomorrow.
                                                    Love, Celia

P.S. We took Mr. Miles with us.

Madeline frowned ruefully at the note, then tossed it int the trash. At least her mother wouldn't be here to scold he and tell her how foolish she was being. Maybe she *was* bein foolish, she thought tiredly. But she would much rather t foolish than sorry.

She made herself some coffee and toast, took a shower and did her hair. All the while she wondered when Jake had found her note and how he had reacted to it.

She didn't want to hurt him; she only hoped he could read between the lines and understand why she had needed to put some distance between them.

The telephone rang just as she was laying down her hairbrush. For a minute she considered not answering it. She was afraid it was Jake and she didn't think she could handle talking to him just yet. But what if he or Celia had been in an accident?

On the fifth ring she lifted the receiver, then just as swiftly wished she hadn't. The caller was Andrew.

"Madeline, how are you?"

The sound of his voice shocked her. She stared at the telephone trying to figure out why he was calling. "Fine, Andrew. And you?"

"So-so," he said. "I tried to get in touch with you yesterday, but there was no answer."

"Oh? Is anything wrong?" she asked.

"No, I just wanted to let you know the house has finally sold. If you'd like to come up today and sign the papers I'll have your check and everything ready. I'm sure you're just as anxious as I am to get all this out of the way."

"Yes, I am. But—today? Is it necessary for me to come today?" She had just ridden a bus for nearly twelve hours. She didn't relish the idea of another trip. All she wanted was to find some quiet place to lie down, someplace where she could think about Jake and the future.

"It's not absolutely necessary," he said. "But I will be leaving town tomorrow for nearly a month, and I thought you'd like to have the money before then."

Madeline didn't want to go, but she knew it would be a relief to get the matter of the house finally settled. Jake's flight, if he still took it, wouldn't get him to Natchitoches until late this evening. If she chartered a plane round-trip she could be back from Ozark before very late tonight. It would be expensive, but now that the house was sold she wouldn't have to watch her pennies anymore.

"All right," she said. "I'll try to be there this afternoon. Where shall I meet you?"

"The office will be closed, so call me at home. I'll drive down and open up."

He sounded pleased that she was coming, but Madeline couldn't have been more unhappy at the idea. "All right, Andrew," she said quickly and hung up the telephone.

Downstairs she scrawled a hasty note, "Gone to Ozark, Madeline," and pinned it to the refrigerator.

As she grabbed her handbag and hurried down the steps, the telephone began to ring again. This time, Madeline didn't hear it. She was already starting her Fiat and heading toward the airport.

Back in Atlanta Jake hung up the telephone with a bang. He couldn't believe she had actually left in the middle of the night, and he cursed himself over and over.

He had talked to Loretta earlier and had managed to piece together what happened. He should never have taken her to his sister's, he thought. He should never have even stopped in Atlanta. He should have known she wasn't ready for the whole family scene!

Jake looked at her note once again, then groaned with despair. They had been so happy that he had thought there would be no danger. Perhaps he should have brought the whole thing out into the open. He should have made her face the fact that she couldn't have children—that *they* couldn't have children, but that they could have each other. The issue here wasn't children, as far as Jake was concerned. He could live without children; he couldn't live without Madeline.

He looked out the window and tiredly rubbed his eyes. Yes, he thought once again, he should have brought it all out into the open, but he had known how sensitive, how vulnerable she was and he had wanted to spare her any kind of pain or sadness.

Damn Loretta for opening her big mouth! Damn Colette for ever being in his past! But damn himself most of all for not handling things the way he should have in the first place!

It was late afternoon when Madeline arrived in Ozark. It had taken the pilot somewhat longer than usual to make the flight because they had flown through a rainstorm. However, the skies began clearing just before they reached town.

At the airport she called Andrew. He was waiting in his car when she arrived in a taxi at his downtown office.

She paid the cabdriver and told him not to wait. The streets were busy with Saturday shoppers and summer tourists. For a moment she watched the traffic, then tapped her toe impatiently and turned to see what was taking Andrew so long.

To her dismay he was studying her through the windshield of his car as though he wasn't quite sure it was really her. Madeline frowned and folded her arms across her breasts. Finally, she saw him reach for his briefcase and climb out of the car.

It was then that she realized how different she must appear to him. Her tight-legged pants and indigo-blue top were certainly not the sort of clothes she used to wear, and her long red hair was windblown and sexily disheveled around her face.

"Hello, Madeline," he said.

"Hello," she responded. She looked at him and felt nothing except distaste.

He acted as though he expected her to say more. When she didn't he unlocked the door and allowed her to enter the office before him.

"I'm glad you could make it," he told her as he sat behind a wide desk.

Madeline took the chair in front of it and crossed her long legs. "As you said, it's important to get this thing settled."

He made no move to get on with business. Instead he folded his hands on the desktop and looked at her, smiling coolly.

"You look—different, flamboyant—I must say. But tanned and beautiful," he told her.

Madeline didn't like his presumptuous attitude. "I've been to the Keys," she explained.

"Oh? Vacation?" he asked curiously.

A surge of warmth ran through her. "No. Honeymoon."

She couldn't have floored him more if she had reached across the desk and slapped him. For once he showed some emotion.

"You're married!"

She saw his gaze fly to her left hand. "Is that so surprising? You're married again."

"Yes, but—you! I thought you didn't like men!" he spluttered.

Madeline looked at him and thought how stupid, how blind and self-absorbed this man was. And to think she had once tried to live her life to please him! To think how she had suffered trying to give him a child!

She suddenly began to laugh. It was as if something was suddenly released from deep within her, and she knew that now she was truly going to be happy. Because as she looked at this man, she kept seeing Jake and she knew that Jake could never be like Andrew. Jake loved her truly and deeply, with all his heart and soul. He wasn't shallow and selfish like this man. He would never reject her because of something she had no control over. They had something special together. Something that Andrew would never know or experience in his whole life.

Andrew's face reddened. Obviously her laughter annoyed him. "You don't have to laugh so brazenly, Madeline. It's just that you turned so withdrawn and cold—"

He broke off as Madeline stared boldly at him. She picked up a pen from a holder on the desk.

"I'm laughing because I feel good," she told him truthfully. "Now would you please gather up the papers. I'm anxious to get back to Natchitoches."

He began to pull out the necessary forms and pointed out the places she needed to sign. Her exotic perfume drifted seductively around her as she examined the papers.

The diamonds shone on her hand, drawing Andrew's attention. He nervously moistened his lips. "Er—Madeline, as I said on the telephone, I'm going to be out of town for a month. Shreveport, actually, just a hop away from Natchitoches. Maybe we could get together."

She looked up at him coldly. He must not care about his new wife any more than he had ever cared about her, she thought. God help his wife and child, because they were the ones who needed it now. Then she thanked God for blessing her with Jake.

"I don't think that would be a good idea, Andrew."

He blanched at her words, but Madeline deliberately ignored him and continued to sign the papers.

"Who's the lucky man?" he demanded. "Anyone I know?"

"You've heard of him. But you don't know him," she said.

"Well, you've managed to make him sound intriguing," he said cattily.

Madeline's smile was wide as she signed the last form. "Jake is much more than intriguing." He was special; he was wonderful!

A little smirk twisted his lips. "Jake?"

"Jake Hunter." She could see the blank expression on his face so she went on. "A.k.a. Harlon Howard. Remember? You were furious because I read his novel *Bitter Harvest*. You said it was nothing but sensual pulp."

"Madeline!" he gasped. "How—"

Before he could go on Madeline said, "If you'll get my check, I'll call a taxi and be on my way."

Reluctantly he handed her the check. "I can drive you to the airport," he suggested.

Madeline began to dial the phone. "No, Andrew. You won't be taking me anywhere."

It was dark and raining when Madeline pulled her Fiat into the driveway. She should have been exhausted, but she wasn't. There was a light on in the cabin and excitement surged through her veins. It was Jake. It had to be!

She ran through the rain to the cabin door. When she opened it and stepped in, Jake was on the telephone.

"Yes—yes that's right," he was saying. "A Fiat—" He must have heard the door close because he suddenly turned to see her standing just inside the threshold. Raindrops glistened on her bright hair and dotted her clothing.

"Never mind," he said woefully into the receiver, "she's here now. Forget the whole thing."

After the receiver landed back in its cradle he began to walk toward her, and Madeline suddenly wondered if it was possible that he could actually look more attractive than she remembered. Though he was probably furious with her, her heart thudded with joy at the sight of him.

"Who was that on the telephone?" she asked.

"The police," he explained. "I wanted to find you."

"Jake," she groaned.

In three strides he was beside her, and he pulled her into his arms. "Madeline, my Lord, why did you leave Atlanta? Why did you go to Ozark? If that—"

Madeline kissed him on the neck, the cheeks, the chin and finally on the mouth. He felt so good to her. He would always feel this good to her. "I left Atlanta because I was confused and hurting," she said sadly. "And I went to Ozark because Andrew called and wanted me to sign some papers. He finally sold the house."

"You saw him?"

She nodded. "Why? Are you jealous?" she asked in disbelief.

"Hell, yes! I'm jealous of anything or anyone that takes you away from me," he muttered roughly, then kissed her hard on the mouth.

Madeline wound her arms around his neck and returned his kiss. She thought she could actually taste the anger, passion and relief he was feeling. Her whole body quivered in response.

Once the kiss was over Jake shook his head and took a deep breath. "No, that's not true, Madeline," he said ruefully. "I was just worried and sick because you left me in Atlanta."

"I didn't mean to hurt you, Jake. I—"

He stepped away from her and began to pace around the small room. "I'm telling you right now, Madeline, I'm going to get this out in the open. Whether it hurts you or whether it might be something you don't want to hear, you've got to face it anyway. This problem is not with me, Maddie," he said. "The problem is with you. You haven't ever faced up to the fact that you'll never have a child of your own. You've hidden the truth away somewhere in a dark place in your heart and until you bring it out and accept it, you'll always be filled with doubts, guilt and self-recrimination.'' He shook his head, and she watched him in silence, knowing he probably needed to say all these things as badly as she needed to hear them.

"My Lord, Madeline. I left Colette because she wasn't the right woman for me. She could choose whether to have a child or not. But she was more concerned about her career. You—you don't have a choice; it was taken out of your hands by someone who knows much greater things than we do. And He put you here for me, Maddie. I know it in my heart. We were made for each other.''

Tears stung her eyes and she ran to him. "I know, darling. I know," she murmured happily, her face crushed against his broad chest. "Today when I saw Andrew I realized how lucky I am to have you, how fortunate we are to have each other. I knew with sudden conviction that you would never be like him, that you'd never blame me for not being able to give you a child. Seeing him somehow released all the old guilt he had filled me with. I know now that as long as you love me I'll have all I'll ever need." She lifted her head to look up at him and smiled through her tears. "I'm a woman. I may not be able to give birth, but I'm still a woman—one who loves you more than any other woman could.''

"You're a special woman," he whispered, his voice rough with emotion. "My woman.''

Jake's woman, she thought joyously. *I'm Jake's woman, now and always.* She lifted her lips to his.

Epilogue

Front Street and the banks of the Cane River were covered with throngs of happy, laughing people. It was the first Saturday of December and every year at this time over a hundred thousand people poured into Natchitoches to attend the Christmas Festival of Lights.

Parades and all kinds of activities had been held during the day. Booths selling everything from food to souvenirs lined the streets. It was a spirited occasion, a time for family gatherings.

Now that darkness had come, the crowd had somehow managed to grow even thicker. Wedged somewhere among the people watching the fireworks was a redheaded woman holding a toddler on her hip. A dark-haired man had his arm around them both. Just to the side of them stood another woman with light brown hair. A tall blond man was by her side, and in front of them stood three boys who were wiggling, shouting and pointing with excitement.

"Look at that one," Michael said with awe, his little finger directed toward the darkened sky over Cane River as a dazzling explosion of color rained down over the water.

"Yeah!" Joel exclaimed. "Mom, Dad, we just got to come to Aunt Maddie and Uncle Jake's next Christmas, too. This is super!"

Madeline laughed as she scooped up a spoonful of the meat pie Jake was holding and fed it to Elizabeth.

"You haven't seen anything yet, boys. Just wait till they turn on the lights. That's the super stuff."

Over 140,000 tiny bulbs and thirty-eight miles of wiring were strung out over many blocks, as well as the bridges crossing the Cane River, and the riverbank itself. When the switch was flipped the whole historic district became a fairyland of lights.

People were shifting behind them, but Madeline didn't notice. She thought it was someone trying to find a better viewing place.

"Madeline, your neon will be lost in the lights tonight," Celia said.

Madeline turned to see that her mother and Charles had managed to find them in the crowd. They all laughed as they looked up at the buildings on Front Street. In one window on the second floor, the word Madeline's was written in colorful neon. Jake had bought the sign for her, saying neon was becoming the in thing again. The dress shop was filled with bright, stylish clothes, and young women had been snatching them from the racks almost as fast as Madeline could put them out.

"For once I won't care, Mother," she said happily. "This is the most beautiful time of the year. My little sign will have its day later."

Loretta reached for Elizabeth. "Here, let me take that weight off you for a while."

Madeline kissed Elizabeth's cheek and handed the child to her mother. Jake put his arm around Madeline's shoulder and grinned down at her. She didn't miss the seductive glint in his eye and it brought a smile to her lips.

"Do you remember when we first came down here on Front Street?" she asked quietly, so that only Jake could hear. "You drove me on the Harley, and I thought you were the most handsome, crazy guy I'd ever seen."

He laughed and nuzzled her ear. "How could I forget? I kissed you for the first time right down there on the riverbank."

She edged closer to him and breathed in his ear. "I wanted you to make love to me. I felt so wanton."

He chuckled huskily. "I'm feeling rather wanton just thinking about it," he whispered back, his finger tracing a circle on her cheek.

Madeline began to giggle and Loretta said, "Did you two lovebirds hear Celia and Charles? They have German chocolate cake, eggnog, date rolls, divinity and all sorts of things waiting for us after the lighting is over."

"Mmm, sounds good," Jake said, casting Madeline a pointed look. She smiled back at him and slipped her hand into his. "I can't wait," she murmured.

Just at that moment the lights were turned on and the crowd gasped. Held close in Jake's arms, Madeline looked at the brilliant displays, then up at Jake's face.

The Christmas lights would shine every night until after New Year's, but she knew the light in Jake's eyes would shine for her always.

*   *   *   *   *

Take 4 Silhouette Desire novels
and a surprise gift
⮞⮞⮞ FREE ⮜⮜⮜

Then preview 6 brand-new Silhouette Desire novels—delivered to your door as soon as they come off the presses! If you decide to keep them, you pay just $2.24 each*—a 10% saving off the retail price, *with no additional charges for postage and handling!*

Silhouette Desire novels are not for everyone. They are written especially for the woman who wants a more satisfying, more deeply involving reading experience. Silhouette Desire novels take you beyond the others.

Start with 4 Silhouette Desire novels and a surprise gift absolutely FREE. They're yours to keep without obligation. You can always return a shipment and cancel at any time.

Simply fill out and return the coupon today!

* Plus 69¢ postage and handling per shipment in Canada.

Clip and mail to: Silhouette Books

In U.S.:
901 Fuhrmann Blvd.
P.O. Box 9013
Buffalo, NY 14240-9013

In Canada:
P.O. Box 609
Fort Erie, Ontario
L2A 5X3

YES! Please rush me 4 free Silhouette Desire novels and my free surprise gift. Then send me 6 Silhouette Desire novels to preview each month as soon as they come off the presses. Bill me at the low price of $2.24 each*—a 10% saving off the retail price. There is no minimum number of books I must purchase. I can always return a shipment and cancel at any time. Even if I never buy another book from Silhouette Desire, the 4 free novels and surprise gift are mine to keep forever.

* Plus 69¢ postage and handling per shipment in Canada.

225 BPY BP7F

Name _____ (please print)

Address _____ Apt. _____

City _____ State/Prov. _____ Zip/Postal Code _____

This offer is limited to one order per household and not valid to present subscribers. Price is subject to change.

D-SUB-1C

COMING NEXT MONTH

#544 THAT'S WHAT FRIENDS ARE FOR—Annette Broadrick
Brad Crawford had once loved Penny Blackwell so much he'd been
willing to let her go. But now Brad was back and determined to save
Penny from marrying the wrong man. After all, to love, cherish and
protect—isn't that what friends are for?

#545 KANE AND MABEL—Sharon De Vita
Kati Ryan's diner was her pride and joy, so sparks flew when Lucas
Kane showed up, claiming to be her new partner. Luke needed a
change of scenery and Kati fit the bill—he'd show her they were both
born to raise Kane.

#546 DEAR CORRIE—Joan Smith
When it came to Bryan Holmes, columnist Corrie James knew she
should take her own advice—"no commitment, no dice." But this
romantic playboy was simply too sexy to resist!

#547 DREAMS ARE FOREVER—Joyce Higgins
Cade Barrett was investigating Leigh Meyers's company for
investment purposes, but in her he found a more valuable asset. He
wanted her for his own, but she'd given up on childhood dreams of
happy endings. He'd have to prove that dreams are forever....

#548 MID-AIR—Lynnette Morland
Whenever Lorelei Chant worked with pilot-producer Chris Jansen,
his sky-blue eyes made her heart soar. The trouble was, Chris seemed
to like flying alone. Could Lorelei convince him that love can happen
in the strangest places—even in mid-air?

#549 TOUCHED BY MAGIC—Frances Lloyd
Architect Alexandra Vickery's new client, Lucien Duclos, was quite a
handful—arrestingly attractive and extremely suspicious of women
designers. Alex was determined to prove herself, but how could she
keep her composure when she discovered he was as attracted to her as
she was to him?

ATTRACTIVE, SPACE SAVING BOOK RACK

Display your most prized novels on this handsome and sturdy book rack. The hand-rubbed walnut finish will blend into your library decor with quiet elegance, providing a practical organizer for your favorite hard-or soft-covered books.

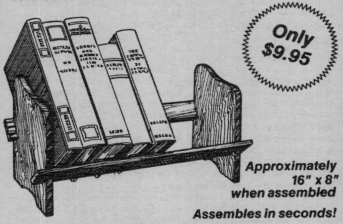

Only $9.95

Approximately 16" x 8" when assembled

Assembles in seconds!

To order, rush your name, address and zip code, along with a check or money order for $10.70* ($9.95 plus 75¢ postage and handling) payable to *Silhouette Books.*

Silhouette Books
Book Rack Offer
901 Fuhrmann Blvd.
P.O. Box 1396
Buffalo, NY 14269-1396

Offer not available in Canada.

*New York and Iowa residents add appropriate sales tax.

BKR-2A

In response
to last year's outstanding success,
Silhouette Brings You:

Silhouette Christmas Stories 1987

Specially chosen for you in a delightful volume celebrating the holiday season, four original romantic stories written by four of your favorite Silhouette authors.

Dixie Browning—*Henry the Ninth*
Ginna Gray—*Season of Miracles*
Linda Howard—*Bluebird Winter*
Diana Palmer—*The Humbug Man*

Each of these bestselling authors will enchant you with their unforgettable stories, exuding the magic of Christmas and the wonder of falling in love.

A heartwarming Christmas gift during the holiday season...indulge yourself and give this book to a special friend!

Available November 1987

XM87-1

Coming in November

Silhouette Classics

You asked for them, and now they're here, in a delightful collection. The best books from the past—the ones you loved and the ones you missed—specially selected for you from Silhouette Special Edition and Silhouette Intimate Moments novels.

Every month, join us for two exquisite love stories from your favorite authors, guaranteed to enchant romance readers everywhere.

You'll savor every page of these *Classic* novels, all of them written by such bestselling authors as:

Kristin James • **Nora Roberts** • **Parris Afton Bonds**
Brooke Hastings • **Linda Howard** • **Linda Shaw**

Silhouette Classics
Don't miss the best this time around!

SCLG-1